Pat Robinson was born in Manchester at the end of World War Two. She took early retirement from being a nursery nurse to travel. It was during her nomadic lifestyle that she wrote The Doll's Hospital trilogy.

Since then she has been a member of various writing groups, one of which was on the Sunshine Coast of Queensland, Australia. She now lives in Yorkshire and is a member of Pickering's Castle Writers.

FRIENDLESS AND BLUE

THE DOLL'S HOSPITAL TRILOGY

FRIENDLESS AND BLUE

HAPPY FAMILIES

THE ATHENAEUM

Friendless and Blue

Book One

of

The Doll's Hospital

CHAPTER ONE

MANCHESTER 1958.

KATHLEEN PEERED out of the window and tried not to look at the reflection staring back. Her haggard face: lined before her years had become painful to see.

Was she tired of running?

Probably, but what was the alternative? The bus pulled into a stop. Immediately her head turned to scan those entering – an obsessive show of nerves – a habit she'd got into during the past three years. His words ingrained into her senses: sharp and menacing as though newly spoken, 'I'll find you Kathleen, no matter where you run, I'll track you down.' And he had.

Soft fingers touched her cheek. Looking down she saw Linda's upturned face and smiled, her gaze loitering briefly before it continued its sweep to rest on her other child, Audrey; her first born who was also scrutinizing passengers travelling their route. *Poor girl* thought Kathleen, eight years old yet she had had no childhood as such: always vigilant, forever taking Kathleen's role, to be her eyes when the need to look elsewhere became necessary. Audrey knew the score; she'd seen Mike's rage many times, felt it once when she ran to protect her mother.

Kathleen settled back into the seat, allowed her lungs to function once more – they were safe, for the moment.

Memories ran like passing trains inside her head. It was becoming harder for her hide. Mike was resourceful, able to use his position as a police officer to seek out the numerous crumbling bedsits she'd been forced to take refuge in. There was the need to earn a living, and to find people she could trust to look after the children whilst she worked. Only for the fact that her skills were in great demand was she able to keep safe, but even then, the tip-off to flee always came from warnings given to her by her careful employers: their fear of losing her etched in their faces as they disclosed that a police sergeant was making enquiries about her. Luckily for Kathleen, the last firm who employed her had connections in Manchester, a sister company so desperate for her skills that they offered her secure accommodation on the premises.

Kathleen jumped at it and a speedy transfer was arranged.

The bus pulled into the next stop, one passenger got off, no one entered, it moved on, she tried to relax – tried to tell herself they were safe now and far away from Leeds – no longer under Mike's radar – no longer fearing his wrath.

It wasn't always so. She gulped back the sadness she felt about their break-up, told herself her children's safety had to come first. He'd begged for forgiveness, and she'd given it so many times believing his rage was an illness but: after the day he used his violence on Audrey; her attitude changed forever. All the passion was gone, the man she once adored, laughed with when he used his clever Northern wit, was gone – now her husband dwelt in shadow – lived in a complex mansion of dark rooms.

During the good times when his dark side stayed hidden, he would speak of his earlier career with the Manchester police force; telling her of the days when he walked the beat with someone called Johnny Johnson. They were good mates then, and long before the injury he'd suffered during a messy arrest. Even as he relayed his hospital experiences Kathleen felt Mike should have been given more time for the healing process to work but his old boss, Sergeant Hammond swung his discharge from the hospital and arranged a clean bill of health for him. Ever since Mike spoke well of Hammond saying he was deeply in his debt for what he'd done.

On the upper deck of the bus a group of children started to sing carols. A pang of guilt gripped Kathleen's heart. She had not told the girls about the Christmas tree in Albert Square and all the lights that would be filling the city's air with festive colour. She knew they would have loved to be taken to see Father Christmas climb down the central dome of Lewis's department store: but how could she dare? Mike would be searching for her even in Manchester. He could be calling in favours, have men tracking her amongst the crowds of shoppers here as well as Leeds or Sheffield.

The bus slowed down as it entered the city's outskirts. It trundled slowly along London Road. Kathleen gathered her things, got up from the seat and rang the bell. According to her directions, their stop was next: the Doll's Hospital was somewhere along a row of terraced businesses that faced the railway station. She took a deep breath – ushered her girls off the bus and opened her umbrella against the seasonal squall.

SUPERINTENDENT HAMMOND of Lever Street police station pulled his collar around his ears and looked down Market Street. He scanned through a sea of umbrellas and tried to ignore the shoppers clutching the hands of children that crowded the pavement eager to enjoy an evening of festive cheer. Hammond suspected that he was being followed but by whom he couldn't say. Thankful that the traffic was slow, he weaved between buses loaded with office workers heading for home, and others bringing in families for the Christmas build up. He glanced behind as he reached the pavement but saw only a happy crowd. The city was booming, and wherever carols were not being sung, music by Johnny Ray was whistled or hummed.

Hammond didn't share the crowd's joy, he merely wanted to serve the needs of his paymaster; the law firm Furnace, Crane and Neilson who in their efforts to defend a gangster called Alfredo Boss, had become a law unto themselves – or so they thought.

Life was becoming tough for Hammond. The new Chief Constable with modern ideas was cause for concern, and with hindsight, Hammond was regretting his idea of persuading Wilson to leave Leeds and be part of his team once more. He worried he'd have to spend more time reining in the manic policeman than letting him off the leash. But, he weighed, he needed someone he could trust and although Mike had deteriorated over the intervening years, he was still the best man for the job.

He ducked into an arcade, pretended to window shop, but used the plate glass to check the crowd behind him. Despite the foul weather, ladies wore sling-back shoes and flimsy swagger coats. They jostled by his side trying to view the latest fashions and cooed with delight at the chiffon cocktail dresses worn by window display mannequins that posed with long cigarette holders; their alabaster faces angled to stare back at the shopper with sophisticated blindness.

Sophisticated blindness, thought Hammond, *there was a lot of that about.* What did the politician say? 'They've never had it so good?' He removed himself from the shoppers, checked his watch, and deciding the coast was clear, headed towards Piccadilly Gardens.

AWAY FROM all the gaiety, the two little girls clung tightly to their mother's coat and strove to keep dry under the precarious angle of her umbrella. Heedless of the slippery pavement, Kathleen walked with speed. The children kept up without complaint, stopping only when she paused to read the brass plates that were fixed to the walls of the offices along London Road. They waited as she scanned, and felt her disappointment before pressing on.

A gust of wind ripped around them turning the mother's umbrella inside out. She struggled to correct it – her blonde curls blowing against the little black feathers of her dainty hat.

With a cry of delight, the youngest child spotted the neon sign, let go of her mother's coat and ran ahead. 'There it is Mummy,' she yelled above the storm, her finger plump with traces of baby fat, pointing to the picture of a doll with its arm in a sling.

Hardened by fear, the mother grabbed hold of the child's gabardine coat and yanked her back. 'What've I told you?' she scorned, looking nervously at each passer-by before lowering her voice, 'I'm sorry luv, but you've got to learn.'

Sorry indeed for her outburst, Kathleen brushed droplets of rain from the child's hood and wished for an end to their terror. Looking up to the entrance before them, she strode the worn steps and when she opened the door – yellow light poured onto the wet stone, lifting them briefly from their gloom. The older child, Audrey, took her sister's hand, gave it a gentle squeeze and led her into the building, closing the door behind them.

Shaking the worse of the wet from their coats, they stood on the large mat and stared up the central staircase – its balustrade spiralling several floors.

'Come on,' Kathleen urged as she made a move to the door on the left, 'and make it sharp.'

Audrey bent to whisper in her sister's ear, 'Look Linda, it says the Doll's Hospital.'

Strident, their mother opened the door, headed for the polished counter and hit the bell with the heel of her hand. At that moment typewriter noises filled the hall behind them catching the girls' attention, they turned, and recognized the silhouette of the man who filled the opposite door's frame. He was preoccupied with tucking an envelope in his inside pocket but when he pulled the collar of the dark raincoat around his ears he looked up and straight into Audrey's eyes.

Before the girl could speak, her mother snatched her from behind, pulled her into the shop and closed the door.

CHARLIE FAULKNER moved unnoticed through the crowds. The man he followed stopped, turned to scan those around him and continued his journey. He's nervous, thought Charlie, pleased the pressure on the senior policeman was beginning to show. The Superintendent stopped at the curb, pulled tight his belt, crossed toward Piccadilly Gardens and gave another furtive glance.

Smiling, Faulkner slid into the scant protection of Lewis's notorious arcade and continued his surveillance. Before long, another man met up with the Superintendent giving Charlie cause to frown. He wore a dark-coat and a trilby hat pulled hard against the wind.

'Well, well,' Faulkner uttered, 'if it isn't our old friend Mike Wilson.' His wiry eyebrows knotted as memories of Wilson's dark deeds flooded back. 'Now,' he whispered, 'I wonder what's brought *you* back to haunt us?'

'Talkin' t'me luv?'

Faulkner spun round.

Hand on hip and dressed in next to nothing, the woman placed one foot on the ledge of the column's plinth and blew a stream of blue smoke from pursed lips. The glossy patent of her shoe and the chain around her ankle picked up the surrounding festive colours, drawing the private detective's twinkling eyes to her shapely leg and pale inner thigh.

'Bloody 'ell Charlie, I didn't recognize yer.' She stamped her foot down and pulled hard on her cigarette.

'You're a bit early Sandra,' his eyes reflecting Christmas twinkle, 'customers looking for what you offer, shop a bit later than this, or am I wrong?'

'No Charlie, you're not wrong but there'll be nowt in their pockets by then,' Sandra shivered, folded her arms across her chest then asked, 'you watchin' anyone I know?'

Charlie stood aside – unblocking her view, 'Ugh,' she snarled, 'might've known – Superintendent 'Ammond, and what's 'e doin' back?' she asked; referring to Wilson.

'Dunno,' twinkled Faulkner, 'but he's going to liven things up around here.'

'Ugh.' Unimpressed, Sandra dropped her cigarette onto the floor and ground it with the sole of her high-heeled shoe. Aware he watched her movement she twisted her ankle from side to side delighting in his smile.

'Get gone girl, go ply your trade whilst you've still got what it takes.'

She gave him one of her best smiles and disappeared into the night. Sandra forgotten, Charlie's attention returned to the policemen. They appeared to be arguing; both oblivious to the wind raging around them, Wilson's agitation was causing his cigarette to spark with mischief above Hammond's uncovered head.

'Dear oh dear Superintendent,' mused Charlie, 'what have you let yourself in for?'

Faulkner sensed the meeting was nearing its end when Hammond attempted to show friendship by slapping his companion's back. Wilson warded him off. His raised arm sent another shower of sparks into the senior policeman's face. He turned into the storm leaving Hammond temporarily blinded. 'Well my lad,' observed Charlie, 'an ill-wind for me but a big mistake for you.' He grinned, made a snap decision and melted into the crowd to follow the new arrival.

A SQUALL of rain hit the roadside window of the Doll's Hospital. A side door behind the counter opened, filling the room with classical music and a man, smaller than the girls' mother, peered over wire-framed spectacles to greet them. 'Good evening Madam.' He scanned the serious face of the customer as another squall of rain rattled the glass of the window. 'Well it isn't really – is it? *Good* I mean,' he chuckled giving each child a friendly wink.

Having neither time nor patience for pleasantries, the mother tipped the contents of her shopping bag onto the counter and pushed them towards him. 'The elastic thing's rotted and needs a new one.'

Oliver Sharples picked up a pink plastic arm noting the scuffed knuckles on the hand. 'If you care to wait, I'll have her fixed in just a few minutes.' He pointed to the green leather seating in the corner of the room.

'As long as it doesn't take longer,' she mumbled, 'I've to be in work by seven.'

Compliant, the doll mender nodded, scooped the dismembered body parts into the black apron he wore and returned to the back room closing the door behind him. In the music's absence, the storm outside demanded full attention with sleet hitting hard against the window.

Kathleen sat down, pulling her children close. Audrey, bursting to tell who she'd seen ventured to speak, but was cut short by the look of warning in her mother's eye. There would be time later when it was safe to talk – meanwhile she looked at the shelves crowded with mended toys awaiting collection by their owners.

MIKE WILSON pushed his way along the pavement, his mood not good, regrets edging into his mind. Hammond had promised good police work, but all he'd been given so far was a list of names – private stuff which Wilson disliked. At the change of lights, he crossed the road and headed towards London Road. The familiar surroundings bringing back memories of the past, to the days when Hammond was a sergeant in uniform and Johnson, a good mate of Wilson, with whom he shared the beat. Now Hammond hobnobbed with judges and politicians – people who paid well for his special services like tracking down witnesses, scaring them into changing their story and tampering with evidence. And Johnson had put an end to their friendship, teaming up with Jenkins, saying he could no longer cope with Wilson's mood swings.

Mood swings – what did they know? It wasn't Johnson who'd taken the blow to the head ten years ago. It wasn't Johnson or Jenkins who suffered the blinding headaches or the probes given by the medics during their experiments. He'd like to sod the lot of them off, but now was not the time. Besides, Wilson never forgot a favour and owed Hammond for the time he juggled the medical records allowing him to walk free from that obscene ward.

He gave a mental shrug – brought his mind back to the present and to where he now was: an all time low if the truth were told and ten years working in Leeds had harvested bugger all. And Kathleen: the final betrayal, had given him the slip and run to ground somewhere in Sheffield.

A nagging thought crept into his head and would not go away. Why had Hammond sent for him to work here, in Manchester – especially as Hammond had transferred him to Leeds in the first place? A smile curved the corner of his mouth, a rarity for a man of his nature. Hammond had lost his cool – he was on edge, always looking over his shoulder. He was still the same selfish man Wilson remembered from years back, just as nasty in a peevish kind of way but now he was scared shitless.

Wilson couldn't help thinking the Super had got himself into something he couldn't handle. He smiled again wondering whether Hammond's paymasters were demanding more of him than he could supply. Or had he been paid in advance but found he could no longer deliver?

Before long, Wilson had climbed the steep hill of the railway station's approach and was stood at the meeting point by the newspaper kiosk – he checked his watch. He'd arranged to meet a Greek seaman – a man trying to protect his family from Hammond's threats.

'Did you speak with him?' The accent was not heavy but the voice was deep. Wilson swung round not expecting such a bold approach. He nodded. 'But no deal eh?'

'No deal – your family must keep to their given story.'

'So the Italian turd can stay out of jail eh?' The seaman reached inside his Reefer jacket, revealed the corner

16

of a package. 'I have money – plenty for you – take it. *You* keep my family safe.'

Wilson shook his head. 'Sorry mate, not my scene – I'm just the errand boy here and the message is, make your family stick to the given statement and no-one gets hurt.'

A crowd of passengers eager to enter the shelter of the station pushed past, the seaman made way for them, Wilson didn't budge.

'But I will be at sea,' the Greek argued, 'with no one to discipline them. They have new hope and for once, they are eager to tell the truth. They want the gangster to go to prison.' He moved aside as more passengers rushed by – behind him a brick hut with steps leading down to the pavement on London Road. The Greek turned towards it and disappeared into the darkness of the stairwell. Wilson moved to catch up.

CHARLIE FAULKNER watched Wilson follow the merchant seaman into the stairwell and ran across the cobbled road to close the gap. At the entrance Charlie heard the seaman's baritone voice echo against the curved brick wall. It threatened and was menacing, even cruel. Wilson wouldn't take much more of this, Faulkner mused as he crept down a step taking each tread at a time. Passengers rushing to the station pushed by – Charlie let them through before edging down the next step.

When he almost reached the bottom, Charlie saw the sailor had Wilson pinned against the wall, he was giving a final warning either to leave his family alone – or to help them. Wilson looked dazed, not in control, allowing the seaman to push him down the rest of the steps and onto the pavement of London Road. Faulkner ran down, tried to follow but the Greek stormed past heading back to the station blending immediately with other commuters.

AS THE rain spattered against the window of the Doll's Hospital, the two little girls stood patiently by their mother's side. Linda turned from gazing at the teddy bears huddled together on the shelf to look at her mother's careworn face. Kathleen sensed her stare and gave a smile slipping a hand around the little girl's dripping coat. Feeling the gentle hug, Linda smiled back, spotted a tattered feather stuck to her mother's forehead and pulled it free.

Music flooded the room when Oliver Sharples returned, holding a large pink doll in the air. 'There she is,' he beamed, 'good as new. Now to which of you does she belong?'

In unison the girls shouted, 'Both of us.'

The door flew open hitting the rubber stopper fixed to the floor. A woman pulling a screaming child and clutching a decapitated teddy bear burst into the room. Wind howled loudly and from the outer hallway, someone yelled, 'shut the bloody door!'

Apologizing, the newcomer ran to push the inclement weather back onto the street; leaving her child performing a tantrum in the muddy puddle the duo had deposited on the linoleum floor. Unused to such ill manners, the two girls watched in horror as the child clambered the panels of the polished counter intent upon reaching its brass bell. A loud slap to the legs brought fresh howls drowning the storm's noise and the music from the workroom. 'Stop it yer little swine, can't ya see the doctor's busy?' placing the soggy teddy and head onto the counter she turned to face the others, giving a weak smile she said, 'he's tired.'

18

With her purse open ready, Kathleen stood up and approached the counter. 'How much do I owe?'

'I'll put it on your next bill.' Oliver said pushing the doll into the scuffed fake-leather shopping bag, drawing the handles together and handing it to the young woman, her cheeks flushed by the kind gesture. Mumbling her thanks, she gathered her children and left the shop. Audrey looked across the hallway to the office and noticed the noise of the typewriters had stopped. Shadows gathered behind the door's glass panel, employees preparing to leave for home. Wind blew rain onto the mat when the mother opened the main door and stepped outside. Audrey took Linda's hand and followed, closing the door behind.

MAKING HIS way onto the pavement Charlie looked amongst the sea of umbrellas battling against the storm. Wilson stood alone: the back of his hand covered in blood as he wiped his nose. In a daze he stared into nothing before he turned towards Piccadilly and slowly headed to where the murky sky was awash with the watery colours of Christmas cheer. Pleased he had something to report to his client, Charlie gave up the chase and headed towards the Waldorf Hotel, his favourite city pub.

HER PACE strident once more, Kathleen headed for the traffic lights, her girls clinging tightly to the hem of her three-quarter-length coat. Workers heading for home stood by the curb waiting for the lights to change. She pushed to the front, peered down the road and glanced at each set of lights. Her bus came into view, her eyes shot back to the lights, *come on* she urged, *let us cross.*

They changed to amber: she stepped off the curb ready to cross but the bus did not stop instead it sailed through leaving a trail of murky moisture in its wake. Her eyes darted to the stop a few yards further along and she was relieved to see a small crowd gathered by it. Again she glanced at the lights but spotted a man with blood streaming from his nose. 'Mike,' she gasped horror filling her senses. Blinking the bus's spray from her eyes, she took another step and with heart pounding, a quick glance to the right judging distances between her and the bus, she ran diagonally into the road, her children in tow. To her left, a taxi travelling behind the bus rolled to a halt but a car travelling too fast clipped the taxi's rear offside and spun out of control knocking the mother to the ground.

Within fractions of heartbeats and screeching tyres, the mother's coat was ripped from the girls' fingers. They made to move towards her, but someone held them back, rushing them away from the hissing, screeching chaos.

CHAPTER TWO

FIRELIGHT DANCED on the crystal lights that hung from the Waldorf Hotel's high ceiling and reflected in the polished mirrored walls of the bar. With the professional ease gained only from years of experience, hotel staff saw to their customer's needs without intruding in their privacy.

Faulkner looked around, noticed his client had not arrived and took off his wet coat. He checked his watch. 'Good evening Mr Faulkner,' the passing waiter greeted – his tray full of empty glasses.

'Evening Kenny, has Mr Gould arrived?'

'Not yet,' the waiter replied, handing a written drinks list to the man behind the bar, 'but it's still early.' Moving to the 'waiter's only' section of the bar, Kenny stacked the empty glasses from his tray, turned to face Faulkner and asked if he would like the usual. Faulkner nodded, hung his coat on the hallstand and took his evening newspaper and brief case to the cosy seating by the fire.

En route to other tables, Kenny placed a soda-siphon by Faulkner's elbow returning a few moments later with a single scotch and a tiny dish of peanuts. Comforted by the familiar surroundings, Faulkner opened the newspaper and settled down to enjoy the warmth of the fire burning brightly in the large marble fireplace.

Whilst the taxi driver ran to the woman's aid, his passenger sped past him towards the row of terraced buildings in search of a telephone. The nearest was behind the counter of the Doll's Hospital where he ignored shouts for him to close the bloody door and the wailing of a child sat with his mother to lift the counter's hatch. He started to dial, the wheel rotating with mind numbing slowness. At last the call was answered and the operator wasted no time in dealing with the emergency.

Oliver Sharples came from the back room and stood by the tall stranger. 'There's been an accident,'the man told the operator, 'an ambulance is needed.' He put his hand over the speaker, 'sorry,' he whispered to Sharples, 'didn't have time to ask permission.' Oliver nodded and walked to the window. Headlights from stationary vehicles lit the scene. Crowds gathered, their silhouettes sending black shadows across the wet paving slabs.

'Yes, ambulance and police are needed,' instructed the city gent. 'Er, one moment,' he turned to Oliver, 'what address is this?'

'Lincoln House.'

'Lincoln House, London Road, opposite the station, yes thank you.' He placed the receiver onto the cradle and held out a hand. 'William Gould.'

'Sharples, Oliver Sharples.' The lean man in pin striped trousers and tailored overcoat, thanked him and raised his bowler to the woman and child before returning to the accident scene where he immediately took charge.

Willing the woman not to die in his arms, the taxi driver sat in the road, handkerchief in hand mopping the flow of blood trickling from her nostrils. Water dripped off the peak of his cloth cap and onto the little black feathers of the hat she wore. Meanwhile Gould cleared onlookers from the road to make way for the approaching ambulance whilst from the opposite direction, the beacon of a police car filled the scene with strobing blue light.

Relieved of duty, Ted threw his rain sodden jacket under the seat of his cab, checked the damage done to his offside lights and hoped the police would allow him to continue with his journey. The ambulance sped away carrying victim and driver with it and much to Ted's relief, the police ordered him to move on. He looked around for his passenger. 'Okay, Mr Gould,' he bellowed above the storm, 'we're free to go.' But Gould, who was stooped with his ear to the mouth of a man wearing a craftsman's apron, didn't hear. With a sigh, Ted crossed the road. 'Come on Mr Gould, we can go.'

'Yes, okay Ted,' Gould straightened, 'before the lady was knocked down,' he enquired of his taxi driver, 'did you notice if she had anyone with her, children say?'

Ted shook his head. 'Can't say, first I knew was my arse-end takin' a wallop.'

'Quite, but Mr Sharples here, says she had two little girls with her.'

'Oi!' one of the officers wearing a large cape came towards them. 'I told you to move on.'

'Come on Sir, this gentleman can sort it out with the police. It isn't our concern.'

Gould nodded, watched Ted return to his cab and reached inside his coat. 'We have to go,' he told Oliver, 'tell the officer what you told me. If you need further advice, here are my details.' He pushed a business card into the doll mender's hands.

Above the noise of the wind and rain, Ted's diesel engine roared into life, Gould addressed the policeman, 'Officer, Mr Sharples here says the accident victim had two

23

children with her.' He nodded for Oliver to continue with his story and headed towards the taxi. An angry roar from the crowd made him look back to where the doll mender lay on the floor, his glasses fallen into his lap and the caped officer pushing pedestrians forcibly away from the scene. 'I say,' Gould ran to Oliver's aid, 'are you alright Mr Sharples?'

'He won't listen to me,' bewailed the little man looking up from the gutter, 'just because I didn't witness the accident.' Gould held out a hand and pulled Oliver to his feet. The taxi rumbled by their side.

'Come on Sir, the police are getting' nowty.' Gould nodded, gave Oliver a gentle pat on the arm and boarded the cab.

Oliver replaced his glasses and stared at the spot where the cab had stood. 'See,' he shouted, stepping across the road unaware of vehicles moving around him. He held the shopping bag in the air. 'See,' a pink doll's head poked over the rim, 'now does anyone believe me?'

CHAPTER THREE

WILSON DUCKED into a shop doorway, cupped his hands around the Ronson and lit a cigarette. Smoke streamed down his nostrils – pressure cracking the bridge of his nose with pain. Bloody Greeks – his mind cursed, bloody Hammond screamed the truth. *That was it* – he'd done with Manchester. Hammond could get someone else to do his dirty work. When he moved, the package the sailor had rammed inside his raincoat, crinkled. He slid a hand inside and felt it – money – a bribe forced on him. Wilson had never taken a bribe in his life. He felt sick.

He pushed the packet back and faced the elements once more – beside him, traffic had slowed, buses with steamy yellow interiors glided by, their ghostly passengers staring out of each window. It was a mistake to come back – he knew that now – renewing relationships never worked. Visions of Kathleen came to the fore. They'd rekindled their love many *many* times – all to no avail. *Oh Mike, I love you.* Crap!

When he turned the corner, a gust of wind blew sparks from his cigarette. As Wilson closed one eye other thoughts opened in his mind. Kathleen giving him the slip in Sheffield had knocked him – some sucker was helping her – had to be. Pain stabbed his ribs, well good luck to him – slag.

25

He took a final drag of his cigarette, tossed it and climbed the steps of the police station.

'Where's Johnson?' he demanded from the young officer working the front desk.

The constable recognised the acting Detective Inspector recently seconded to C.I.D. and gave him a smile, 'traffic accident Sir, taken Jenkins with 'im.' Returning to his paperwork the young man enquired, 'settling in okay?'

'What's it to do with you?' Wilson snapped, 'I worked this beat when you were in nappies.'

The young constable's cheeks coloured, 'I only asked,' he said and turned his back on Wilson to continue with his work.

Brocklehurst, the station's official front desk officer approached the counter, 'Everythin' okay Brown?'

'Yeh Sarge.'

'Good, then arrange some transport to take Hutton to the infirmary, he'll be at the back door in five minutes.' Brocklehurst looked over his shoulder, gave Wilson a curt nod. 'You finished 'ere?' He asked, waiting for Wilson to leave. 'Or there again,' Brocklehurst leaned towards Wilson, 'you've a car, haven't yer?' Wilson nodded, 'Then *you* can run Hutton to the hospital.'

TED TURNED off the engine and settled back. Other passengers had booked him and he worried he was running late. The police were not going to allow him to wait by the roadside for long but Mr Gould did have a point. They *were* ignoring the little man's concern over two little children.

A loud bang echoed from the roof of his cab. He looked up and into the face of one of the policemen as he approached the driver's side. Wearily, he wound down the window, rain sprayed in, adding to his previous soaking.

'You've been told to move on. With or without your passenger I want this cab away NOW.'

The rear passenger door opened and Mr Gould got in. 'It's okay officer. Come on Ted, you were right, we've outstayed our welcome.'

Ted dropped his passenger outside the entrance to the Waldorf Hotel and sped away. Gould caught sight of Faulkner and the eye of the waiter. He took off his coat, hung it to dry and crossed the busy lounge.

'Sorry I'm late Charlie, got caught in a traffic accident.'

The weather-beaten private detective looked up from his newspaper. 'You okay?'

'Yes, but a woman was knocked down. Pretty nasty affair.' The waiter put a glass of whiskey on the table and carried on to tend to other customers. Gould placed the glass under the siphon, gave it a shot of soda and took a drink. 'Ah, that's good.'

Charlie Faulkner folded his newspaper and put it aside. 'I've got some news for you.'

Gould took another sip of the pale liquid. 'The police handling the accident were bloody rude.'

Eager to pass on his latest snippet Faulkner coughed and repeated his declaration. Gould looked at the private detective. 'Oh I'm sorry Charlie, what did you say?'

'Hammond's brought Wilson back.'

Back on track, Gould's clear blue eyes snapped into focus. 'Wilson? But he can't possibly be of help to Hammond. Not at this stage of the proceedings, anyway.'

'I know and unless he's changed, Wilson will drive Hammond to slip up. Then we'll have him.'

Faulkner brought his client up to date. 'The Greek tried to bribe Wilson, but I don't think it'll work. Wilson's never been money oriented.'

'There'll be no need for bribes when we get Alfredo into court. Those days are over. This time the witnesses will tell the truth and he'll go to prison, together with Hammond and the rest.' Gould gave Kenny the nod. 'By the way, Alfredo's been absent for too long, when did you say he's due back?'

'Bernardo wants him out of the way and I don't blame him. He's extended Alfredo's stay in London for as long as he could. I've had an eye kept on him, but he's not got up to much; just visited old haunts in the boxing world, that sort of thing. I'm informed he's due back any day and, as Hammond hasn't been successful in reining-in the witnesses, Alfredo won't be too pleased.' Both picked up their nearly empty glasses and drained the contents. 'So,' Charlie leaned forward, 'tell me about the accident and how you got involved.'

OLIVER SHARPLES returned to the Doll's Hospital down-hearted and thoroughly soaked. He took off his apron and hung it over a chair back. The attitude of the policemen was both disturbing and annoying, where had common courtesy gone? The necessity to clear the road and return the traffic to normality, he understood, but surely two missing children took priority?

Parcels stacked on the corner of his workbench reminded him he had a business to run. Donning his overcoat and hat, he took the packages, locked up shop and headed for the Central Post Office. Expecting to see huddled children in every corner – his eyes searched the basement steps of each business along his terrace. He tried to brush away morbid thoughts: perhaps their mother had someone else with whom the girls could be with; perhaps their father had taken them for instance? Yes, he told himself, he let out a pent-up sigh, that's it. They're safe at home with their daddy.

On his return the breakdown truck loaded with the wrecked car was pulling away and final bits of debris were being swept up. Anxiety crept back, upsetting his thoughts once more. He had seen the faces of the children light up at the sight of their repaired doll. A doll shared by both – much played with and loved. A doll with scratched knuckles and knees would not be left behind. Oliver's logic told him that if the girls were safe with their daddy, then why hadn't they taken their beloved doll with them?

IN THE passenger seat of Wilson's car Constable Hutton chatted on – in his opinion, police methods had changed for the worse. 'Y'know Sir, your reputation is legendry. Some of the old coppers insist the streets were a bloody sight safer for kids when you walked the beat. Can't tell you how proud I am to work alongside you.'

Wilson let him prattle – his mind on their destination and the pulse throbbing in his ears. Oh he was happy to drive the constable around, anything was preferable to Hammond's bloody jobs – but how was he going to bring himself to enter the doors of another hospital? Even the smell of the places reduced the contents of his bowel to liquid.

'The number of molesters is increasin' I'm sure of it – why only last month Billy Quince got off with a technicality, bloody disgra….'

'I'll drop you off at the main entrance,' Wilson interrupted, rain pounding the car's roof. 'I'll find somewhere to park then catch you up.' He drove through the Infirmary's open gates, headlights sweeping the cream stone and red brick façade. 'Place hasn't changed much,' he said as his companion closed the door with a bang and headed for the cover of the entrance.

Sweat trickled through Wilson's scalp. Griping pains shot across his abdomen, he turned, heading back to the toilet. What the hell was keeping Hutton? How long does it take to get a couple of statements? He washed his hands, followed the signs for the ward and stood by the doors. Hutton was by the Sister's desk, they chattered in whispered tones. Wilson crept in, gave Hutton a grunt to hurry up, and leaned against the wall unable to enter further. The Sister inclined her head towards a side-room, Hutton followed her gaze – their conversation too low for Wilson to hear but he understood the room must contain someone involved in the accident. Lazily his vision drifted to the room, and through the door's window to a coat hung to dry behind a bedside locker. He straightened and starred at the grey tweed – his mind reeled *Kathleen.*

'She's not here.' The Sister's voice made Wilson jump. He didn't remember crossing from the exit and standing by the sideward door. 'She's being prepared for theatre.' The smell of starch in her uniform filled his blood-encrusted nostrils – bile burnt the back of his throat. The telephone rang, she ran to answer leaving Wilson staring into the side room.

Hutton joined him and spoke in hushed tones. 'We've no information on the victim yet, Sir. The Sister's got 'er purse an' things.' Wilson nodded, gave the door a light push and walked in. 'So if it's okay Sir? I've done 'ere if you want to leave – I'll just say thanks.'

Left alone, Wilson reached out to touch the coat's fabric and swallowed. It was very like Kathleen's but hell, there must be hundreds similar to this. Hutton's words rang in his mind *her purse an' things*. His phobia of hospitals forgotten, he ran to the Sister's desk and asked to see the purse. Still in conversation on the telephone, she opened a cupboard by her knee and passed it to Hutton. Wilson stared at the purse – no, it was far too ugly for Kathleen. His wife had taste, wouldn't be seen dead with crap like that. Shaking his head, he turned to go, the need to leave the hospital returning with urgency.

Wilson left the ward. Along the corridor two porters wheeled a patient into the lift. He caught a glimpse of the face as the doors closed and for the second time that evening his mind reeled. *Kathleen!*

SERGEANT JOHNSON drove the police van into the parking spot and pulled on the handbrake. Jenkins lit two cigarettes, handed one to his colleague and they sat listening to the rain pound the roof of the vehicle. Men of little words they mulled over the evening's work, Johnson pleased the traffic was quickly put on the move, Jenkins counting the days to his retirement. The beams of a car's headlight swept their van and came to a breakneck halt by the police station's back door. 'Bloody 'ell that's all we need.'

Wilson slammed his car door and headed towards them his face contorted with familiar signs of rage. Jenkins wound the window down. 'What d'ya want Mike?'

'The accident – what did the woman look like?'

'Mangled an' bloody – what the 'ell d'yer think she looked like?'

'Did she have any kids with her?'

'Don't you start,' groaned Johnson, 'we've had a belly full of that already.'

31

Jenkins opened the door deliberately knocking it into Wilson. 'Piss off Mike. Go get 'Ammond to find yer sommat t'do.'

Johnson got out, opened the back doors and started to unload. 'Yeh get 'im to find a nice little priest for yer to get yer fists into.'

Little priest? Why did they delight in bringing up the past? Wilson stood in the pouring rain whilst Jenkins helped his mate clear the van – they worked well together, reminding Wilson of the days when Johnson and *h e* had a similar rapport.

'You still 'ere?' Jenkins sneered as he carried a box towards the station's back entrance. Wilson shrugged, Jenkins was a little shit, always had been, the shrug crinkled the envelope tucked snug and dry inside his coat. Hammond. Wilson's mind flashed, he would be waiting for his report – without a word he shot past the uniformed police and headed towards the Criminal Investigation Department of the building.

JOHNSON APPROACHED the desk, 'Okay lad,' he whispered to Constable Brown.'I want you to put this somewhere safe – somewhere away from prying eyes – got it?' The desk officer took the box, looked twice at the pink doll and before his lips formed any words. 'No funny remarks,' warned Johnson, 'we're not in the mood. Just keep it hidden – no matter who asks. Okay?' Brown nodded, found a place in the stationery cupboard and locked it. Satisfied, Johnson followed Jenkins down to the canteen where the pair could take off their waterproofs, enjoy a dry cigarette and a cup of hot sweet tea.

THE CRIMINAL Investigation Department was a recent extension to the old police station and had the benefit of large modern windows. At that time of night these took on a mirrored effect thus doubling the room's size. Back to back grey metal filing cabinets separated the room into two halves; with Superintendent Hammond's glazed office positioned on the sidewall facing the main door. No one entered of left without his noticing. The door slammed shut, Wilson marched in and entered the Super's office without the customary knock.

'Bitten off more than you can chew with this Greek.' He told Hammond pointing to the blood congealed around his nose.

Hammond stretched his podgy neck, checked whether anyone was within earshot and whispered, 'Not here, you idiot, did you give him my message?'

'Oh yeh – he's so scared, he smashed me fuckin' nose.' He pulled the package out and handed it to Hammond. 'Ses there's more if you leave his family alone.'

Shocked at the sight of the package, Hammond pushed it back, stood up and looked around the office.

Wilson had never seen him so agitated. 'Jesus – what the hell's getting to you?'

Beads of sweat dotted the Superintendent's shorn scalp – he's not well, thought Wilson replacing the package inside his raincoat.

'Meet me at the Royal in an hour,' whispered Hammond his eyes darting back to the main door, 'can't talk here.'

'I'm not staying – thought I'd let you know. I'll return to Leeds at the end of the week.'

'Plain clothes doesn't appeal then?'

'Working for gangsters and pimps doesn't appeal.'

Despite the mirth created by Hammond's anxiety, Wilson was sickened by the man's fear. He felt used. Without another word he slammed out rattling the glass in the office door. The bridge of his nose ached, his ears throbbed and his mind reeled with images of a patient on the hospital trolley. Sense told him it wasn't Kathleen; his mind played tricks all the time, fooling him into seeing her everywhere. Yet there was *something* about the woman's face.

CONSTABLE BROWN stood up to the acting Detective Inspector who had been rude to him earlier and refused to show him details of the accident. 'They're not ready,' he told Wilson, 'Sergeant Johnson's given strict instructions no one's to touch 'em.'

'Listen you little shit…'

'Everythin' alright Brown?' Brocklehurst approached the desk, 'ah, it's Wilson again. I 'ear uniform isn't good enough nowadays – Italian suits made by gangster's yes-men for you from now on is it?' The burly officer leaned across the counter's top, 'take some advice from an old hand and acquire some listening skills before rushing into unchartered waters, and …' Wilson rushed off before Brocklehurst could finish.

The burley desk Sergeant gave the constable a knowing wink, 'not to worry lad, we'll soon be shot of 'im – he's only 'ere on a temporary transfer.'

'WHAT DID you mean when you said you'd already had a belly full of that?' Johnson and Jenkins looked up from their steaming mugs and groaned.

'Piss off,' said Jenkins.

'I want to know what you meant,' Wilson said pulling up a chair.

'What you on about? That scar on your skull givin' you the gyp?'

Ignoring Jenkins's comments Wilson turned to Johnson, 'I asked if the woman had kids with her and you said…'

Jenkins interrupted, 'we'd had enough with the bloody doll mender.'

'Doll mender?' Wilson turned back to Jenkins. 'What's a fucking doll mender to do with my wife?'

Johnson took an intake of breath and moved his pack of cigarettes away from Wilson's coat sleeve, where water dripped off the cuff, forming a puddle. 'Mike? Where've you been to get so wet?'

'Walking - needed to think – answer me, did the woman have any kids with her?'

'What's this about your wife?' Johnson's voice soft, calming, reassuring to Wilson's ears, always had been: ever since the early days Johnson had managed to soothe Wilson's temper, calm him down.

'I think it was her got knocked down tonight.'

'No mate,' Johnson soothed, 'she's not your wife.'

'How d'you know? You've never met her.'

It was true; after the split, Hammond pulled strings and had Wilson transferred. Years passed before news came he'd married a Yorkshire lass.

'I'm just sayin' she can't be your wife that's all, if you don't believe me, nip over to the Infirmary, tek a look for y'self.'

Wilson put the offered cigarette to his lips noting how steady his former colleague's hand held the lighter.

'Already been, drove Hutton there, think I recognised her coat.'

'Didn't get a close view then?'

'No.' Smoke streamed from both nostrils, the puddle forming by his sleeve growing.

'Why don't you take your coat off Mike?'

'Because 'e's not stayin' that's why!' roared Jenkins. 'Don't encourage 'im: 'e's nowt but bloody trouble. Why the 'ell 'Ammond brought 'im back I'm buggered to know.' Jenkins rose from the table, took his mug of tea to another and sat down.

Wilson continued to ignore Jenkins. 'Tell me, did she have any kids with her?' he asked Johnson, his voice trembling with weariness.

'No she didn't.' He gave long sigh. 'There was a ghoul – y'know we always get 'em creeping around disasters. Anyway he didn't even witness the crash, wasn't anywhere near when it 'appened – but appeared from nowhere wanting me to hold the traffic up all night, insisting she had a couple of kids with 'er.'

'If it is Kathleen, then she would have a couple of kids with her – two girls.'

Johnson nodded, 'yeh, if she was your wife, but she isn't. Your wife's in Yorkshire mate, what reason would she have to come 'ere?'

Jenkins re-joined them. 'I'm off,' he said collecting his waterproof jacket, 'leave you to tie up the loose ends Johnny.' He turned to address Wilson. 'From what I 'ear, your wife's better off without you.'

Without taking his eyes off Wilson, Johnson nodded, 'Yeh Jim, see yer tomorrow,' he lowered his voice, 'look Mike, your missus leaving you is nowt to do with us but I can assure you, she wasn't knocked down tonight. Why don't you go back to Yorkshire?'

Running fingers through his thick hair, Wilson stifled the tremble he felt in his breathing and pulled hard on the cigarette. 'When Hammond asked me back, I thought we could be mates, like before, but he's so deep in shit…'

'Yeh an' if you're not quick witted, he'll drag you in it.' Johnson interrupted.

'What does he want from me?'

'Dunno. Me an' Jim don't 'ave that much to do with 'im any more. Most of 'is work comes via that bent law firm, Neilson something or other,' Johnson pulled his chair closer, 'they owe 'Ammond plenty, if y'know what I mean – remember when you raided that brothel after being given the tip off little lads was being buggered?'

'Yeh?' Wilson never forgot a case of child abuse.

'Well we think 'Ammond saved the skin of a couple of judges by givin'em advance warning of the raid.'

The throb in Wilson's neck started to thump. He knew at the time, the net should have caught bigger fish. It made sense – Hammond would have seized the opportunity to win over powerful clients – but to let perverts go? Perverts set free to continue their vile pursuits! As he listened to Johnson's voice, the soothing effect faded replaced instead by a pulse inside his head thumping and throbbing loud in his ears leaving his mind filled with horrors of the past.

'One of the law firm's clients,' Johnson continued, 'a gangster named Alfredo Boss, remember 'im?' Wilson pretended he didn't, wanting to learn what Johnson knew, and shook his head. 'Probably not on your patch,' Johnson reasoned, 'anyway, 'e's about to stand trial for fraud an'Ammond's got to try to get him off. Otherwise...,' Johnson made a cutting sign to his throat.

'This anything to do with a Greek seaman?'

'Dunno, could be – he's into all kinds of shit.'

Johnson's right, thought Wilson – Hammond's up to his fat neck. 'What's this to do with Hammond bringing me back? He's managed well enough so far.'

Johnson shrugged his shoulders. 'Dunno mate, but 'Ammond could be looking for a scapegoat, someone to take the spotlight off 'im. Or, might actually *think* you could be of help,' he stifled a laugh, 'only kiddin' but listen, 'Ammond looks after 'imself.   Go back to Leeds where you've mates who know nowt about this crap.'

'And what if it's Kathleen up there in the Infirmary? Don't I have the right to find out who she's shacked up with?'

'It's not her – an' even if it is, isn't she entitled to her own life?'

Wilson leapt to his feet knocking the table.   Water poured over the edge and onto Johnson's lap.

'Shit Mike, you've just soaked the only part of me that was dry.' He stood up, shook away the excess water and looked up. Wilson had left the canteen. Weary and tired, Johnson gathered his cloak and headed to complete the accident's paperwork before going home.

WHEN WILSON enquired, the patient was still in theatre; he didn't leave his name but said he'd telephone later. He drove around the city, slowing at the traffic lights where the accident had taken place. He and the Greek had argued just feet from the lamppost now twisted due to the impact of the car. The accident had happened moments after he left. If the seaman hadn't been so bloody quick-fisted, Wilson might have seen the woman: then he'd know if it was Kathleen.

He checked his watch – shit, he was late for Hammond. As he drove towards the Royal, Wilson's stomach churned with an old yearning, a feeling he'd not had for a while. According to Johnson, amongst Hammond's clients were perverts, some judges, and who knows what else? Instead of jacking it all in, he could stay on, find out how many Hammond had shielded and track them down, one by one. Now – thought Wilson - that *was* his forte.

Few vehicles stood in the rear car park of the Royal Hotel; none of which Wilson recognised as Hammond's. He stormed into the pub – looked around for the Super, realised he'd missed him and returned to his car. His mind flitting from Hammond's clients to the patient undergoing an operation, he didn't bother to look up when someone asked for a light, but reached instead for his Ronson.

OLIVER SHARPLES paced the floor of his hallway. He had not slept well. It was too early for the morning papers and the radio gave no mention of missing children. He stared at the business card given to him by the taxi passenger and Gould's words echoed inside his head – '*If the police don't take you seriously, let me know.*' They hadn't taken him seriously, despite the calls he'd made to the station. Pushing his spectacles up his nose he started to dial Gould's home number.

'Alderley Edge double five two one, Cynthia Gould speaking.'

'Hello, my name is Oliver Sharples – can I speak to Mr Gould?'

'A moment please,' he heard her call the name William, mention Oliver's name and the phone click when he answered.

'I know it's early, but the police don't intend to search for the children. They say it was just a traffic accident.   Surely they could do more? I see from your card that you know the law. I need advice as to what to do next.'

'Give me your telephone number,' Gould replied, his manner terse yet polite, 'I'll get back.'

WHEN WILSON came too – he was sat in the passenger seat of his own car – the packet of money firmly positioned on his lap. Outside, the racket of draymen delivering barrels of beer to the Royal Hotel's cellars informed Wilson that although dark, it must be morning. Running fingers over a sore spot he found the lump on the back of his head, not in the exact place of his old wound, but close. He stared at the package resting on his knee. Tilting it towards the streetlight, and read the scribbled message not intended for himself but for Hammond. He climbed into the driver's seat and switched on the engine. None of the draymen looked up as the car slid silently from the car park and onto the road. Flicking on his lights Wilson headed straight for his digs – he needed to wash and change before confronting Hammond – and this time, he was not going to be fobbed off by his paranoia.

The scene at Lever Street Police Station and presence of two parked up limousines, complete with uniformed drivers, warned Wilson to back away. Top brass making a visit at that time of the morning could only mean one thing. They were onto Hammond already. Involuntarily a smile cracked his sore and swollen upper lip. Bloody hell, he thought, I can just picture the little prick – sweating like a pig and squealing his innocence. He drove down a side street and parked out of sight wondering if Hammond's counter-part in uniform had also been rumbled. Benson had been on the fiddle for years – though not in Hammond's league. Wilson used the phone box to enquire about the traffic victim and was told she was very poorly but stable. He hung up when asked if he was a relative and returned to his car.

HEAD OFFICE'S sudden interest in a traffic accident had officers of Manchester's second largest police station in a stir. In the first floor conference room, a special meeting was taking place. Attended by senior offices from both uniform and C.I.D., the air was prickly with accusation. And high-ranking officers from Minshull Street were there to ask why a member of the public's concern for two missing children had been ignored. Among those summoned to attend was Superintendent Hammond – not pleased to have his department brought into focus, he fumed in silence as the Chief Constable warned of complacency and sloth; and groaned inwardly when he realised that before attending the unscheduled meeting, who he'd handed the case to.

Detective Inspector Ian Clayton was not one of Hammond's best men, oh yes he got results, eventually – but his manner, his approach to his work was, well – scruffy. He looked as though he slept in his suit, and even after having a week's leave; he appeared underfed and badly shaved. Hammond felt the eyes of the Chief Constable on him, whose words had moved on from taking the job for granted to taking bribes. Was he referring directly to him? The senior officer turned his direction to the uniform section and addressed Benson. Hammond let out a breath – so it wasn't just in his mind – he really could feel them closing in. After making his point, the Chief Constable ended the meeting by insisting that every effort be made to identify the victim and find her children.

41

SATISFIED THE police were about to search for the little girls at last; Oliver Sharples took an early train into the city arriving at the Doll's Hospital just as the cleaners were finishing for the day. He closed his ears to their complaint of mud encrusted counters and dirty footmarks all over the stairs and landing – their language too colourful for his taste.

Inside his workroom – he made a cup of tea and tried to set his mind to mending toys. His nerves were jaggy – even the radio's music too jaunty for his taste. He turned it off and reached into the box for the toy marked first on his repair list. It was wet. Pulling the box to him he felt another – it too was wet. He looked up and saw the dark stain on the ceiling.

DETECTIVE INSPECTOR Ian Clayton reached for his well-thumbed street map. He found the page he wanted and traced a long finger indicating the spot where the accident had happened.

'Okay Davies pay attention, a taxi enters London Road and stops at the lights here,' he waited for his constable to catch on, 'a car travelling behind clips the taxi's rear, spins out of control and knocks down a female pedestrian here.' Pointing to a few notes on his desk he added, 'apparently, this woman had two children with her, yet not one of these statements mention them.'

Detective Constable Davies looked up from the map. 'The weather was 'orrible Sir, maybe folk were tryin' to get out of the rain and not lookin' down where littl'uns tend to be.'

'Perhaps they were but these statements are sketchy, they tell us bugger all.' Clayton placed a piece of paper over the page and traced an outline of the road and surrounding buildings. 'We've lost time on this; need to recall the memories of those people who crossed the road when the accident took place.' He checked his watch, 'Most will be making the return journey to work, clear it with B.B. and take a couple of uniformed officers to those traffic lights. Question travellers as they wait on the curb, find out what time they crossed last evening, I want statements from those five minutes before the accident – they could have seen the woman and her children: jog their memory but don't put words in their mouth.' Clayton pencilled an arrow indicating the premises on London Road. 'And, I want to know if anyone saw the accident from these windows – check the offices, businesses along this terrace.'

Davies drained his mug of tea, pulled on his overcoat and prepared to leave. 'I suppose uniform went to the 'ospital last night. Didn't the woman 'ave an 'andbag or owt?'

Clayton sighed. 'I don't know what uniform found Davies; I'm on my way to the hospital now. If *owt* can be found, then let's call it a start.'

FOR ONE brief moment, the Infirmary's façade was lit by a rogue ray of sunshine cheering Clayton's spirits before a cloud repaired the slit and plunged the city back to winter's gloom. By the entrance, a little flower hut filled the air with perfume; he breathed in the scents and made his way through the huge iron gates. A porter directed him to the ward where the Matron greeted him, took him to one side and spoke in whispered tones.

'She can't help you Inspector, she hasn't regained consciousness *and* I'm afraid she's slipping fast.'

Clayton nodded. 'We need to go through her personal possessions. A witness has come forward stating there were two children with her at the time of the accident.'

She checked the night shift's diary. 'Ah yes, that'll be the man who telephoned last night,' she said. 'He phoned again this morning but we couldn't help him.' She picked up a neatly folded stack of clothes and placed them in front of Clayton. 'Her things,' she said, noting how long he studied the many times repaired shoes and the little back hat. She liked the line of his lean jaw and cheekbones and the way his blue-black bristles threw a *seven o'clock shadow* under his chin.

He turned back to her and gave a smile. 'Is there a handbag or purse?'

She passed a large purse to him. 'Her coat's hanging here, still soaked,' she pointed to a grey tweed coat hooked on the corner of a locker door.

Stuck to the lining of the coat's pocket, Clayton found two soggy bus tickets; he peeled them off and put them aside. In the other he found a sixpence and a threepenny bit, which he placed by the purse on the Matron's desk.

'Was there a handbag?'

'No,' she sighed, 'all you see is what she had on her, oh and this crumpled umbrella.' She pointed to a mess of spokes and black silk on the floor by the locker. 'Please take it with you, I keep thinking it's a dead bat.' He smiled again, 'You've got dimples,' she said.

'So I've been told.' He scooped the contents into an envelope. 'She doesn't appear to have a key.'

The Matron shrugged her shoulders. 'Maybe she has someone at home.'

'Then why haven't they reported her missing?'

'Good point,' she removed the stack of clothes from her desk. 'Is there anything else, Inspector?'

'No, thank you, but I'm surprised uniform didn't take these back to the station, last night.' He picked up the purse and envelope.

'According to Sister Kendal the constable was very considerate when he took statements and he did ask to see the purse, but had to leave in a hurry because his driver had parked too close to the entrance, or something.'

A BAD atmosphere hung around Lever Street Police Station, no one gave Clayton eye contact as he walked through the main office and men known to be work shy were unusually engrossed in paperwork. As his hand reached to push open the door to the Criminal Investigation Department a warning in the form of Davies's voice rang in his head, *I don't like it Sir, summat's up,* the voice said and taking a deep breath, Clayton uttered to himself, 'nor do I lad, nor do I.'

The colour of his boss's skin confirmed the feeling of foreboding and Clayton braced himself to expect a tirade of abuse. As he tipped out the contents of the envelope he'd brought from the hospital, his mind ticked off the countdown sequence before a dynamite blast, *five, four, three, two…..one.*

'Clayton: my office NOW.'
Bang on cue.

Clayton preferred to keep open the Super's door when ordered to the glazed office. This being no exception, he stood in the frame and looked onto the purple skinned head of his boss. Sweat dotted the roots of his short fair hair and brow. Without looking up, Hammond snarled, 'tell me what you know about this bloody traffic accident.'

'The lady's in a bad way, the witnesses need to be re-questioned and we've lost fifteen hours of detection work.'

45

Hammond studied the paperwork on his desk, making no sign he'd heard Clayton's words. After a moment Clayton continued, 'D.C. Davies is gathering what information he can from the scene and I've just returned from the hospital with the woman's purse.'

Hammond raised his head; his pale eyes studying Clayton's off the peg suit with distaste. 'And what progress on the missing children?' he asked.

'With due respect Sir, uniform should have....'

'I'm not interested in what uniform should or should not have done, that's for Benson to deal with. My concern is with the Chief Constable and his meddling in my department.'

'Then I'd better not waste time, Davies is due back soon and, with luck we'll have a trail to pick up.' He turned to go.

'Oh and I suppose that means plodding around town for bloody hours, getting nowhere?' His pale lashes moved slowly as he studied Clayton once more, 'just look at you, you're a bloody disgrace and when are you going to buy a decent razor?' he returned to reading the paperwork on his desk. 'Get out.'

Able to keep his personal feelings to himself Clayton documented the contents of the purse. Inside the wallet section he found a receipt for something costing four shillings and eight pence, a ticket for the washhouse and a ten-shilling note. Clayton jotted the washhouse address in his diary, placed it with the bus tickets inside his wallet and left the building where cool moist air filled his lungs as he walked along the city's pavements.

In the district of Gorton opposite the famous Belle Vue Zoological Gardens and Pleasure Park, the Corporation owned washhouse stood between the public baths and the indoor swimming pool (temporarily closed as fear of another polio outbreak swept the area).

The partially covered entrance was cluttered with old prams. Their purpose to carry the families' washing or any other cumbersome load, their storm aprons and hoods tightly fastened to keep out the rain. A mixture of hot linen and steamy detergent assailed Clayton's nostrils as he opened the main doors and looked for someone in charge. Silver steel appliances reflected in the quarry-tiled floor and women with rolled up sleeves laughed at jokes told over sinks of steaming, soapy suds.

'Can I 'elp yer luv?' a voice shouted above the din.

Clayton turned towards it and looked down at a little woman wearing a green overall and Wellington boots; her hair wrapped turban-style in a cotton headscarf.

He showed his warrant and the ticket. 'I need to know the name and address of this lady,' he yelled above machinery noise. The little lady took the ticket, tilted it to the light and squinted. Shaking her head she beckoned another woman to join them.

'I don't work on a Wednesday,' she confided, 'but Jan's done a couple of stints for 'er mam.'

Jan looked across, placed a freshly ironed sheet on the bench and walked towards them. 'What's up Peggy?'

'Police Inspector,' Peggy shouted above the noise of the machines. She passed the card to Jan. 'Wants ter know whose ticket this is.' She turned to Clayton. 'Yer see, everyone pays when they book so we don't keep a tag on their name or address; if they don't turn up then it's their lookout.'

Jan shook her head as she scrutinized the ticket. 'Can't remember, butta'think she's that new lady – got a posh pram. Dot or Alice'll know 'er.' She pulled a wristwatch from the top pocket of her overall; 'Dot's at the brickworks, but Alice'll be at the Lake now.'

'The Lake?'

'Yer know, the pub,' she took Clayton by the arm and led him outside. 'See, yer can't miss it,' she said pointing the detective in the right direction.

Jan watched him walk away.

Peggy joined her.

'Well Peggy, he's a bit of alright – eh?'

'Nah – too thin fer my taste.'

'I like 'em lean – butta'bet that bloody Alice offers to fatten 'im up.'

LOST IN a world of puppets, the ballet and the theatre, Oliver Sharples placed the blade of his chisel against the piece of timber held in the grip of his lathe. He hummed as shavings of toffee coloured wood curved away, falling onto the floor as the timber rotating before him transformed into the shape of a marionette's new limb. Above the whine of the motor he heard the shop's bell ring, switched the machine off and turned to attend to the customer. Before he reached his workshop door it opened.

'Good morning Sir, I'm Detective Constable Davies.'

'Oh yes,' said the doll mender, taken aback by the directness of the young man. 'Do come in.'

'Thank you Sir, my, but it's nice and warm in 'ere,' said Davies taking off his overcoat and placing it on the back of Oliver's chair.

'Er, would you like a cup of tea?'

''Ow kind – I take two sugars.' Davies made himself comfortable.

'Yes, er please, do sit down. I'll er, put the kettle on.'

Davies stared around the workshop, his eyes resting on two soft toys tied by their ribbons to dry. 'My my Sir, naughty teddies – was it an 'angin' offence eh?'

'The flat above has sprung a leak,' said Sharples his voice showing disappointment at Davies's youth. 'Anyway, I've informed the letting agents – that's all I can do. Best if these things are dealt with immediately, don't you think?'

'Not your problem Sir if you don't mind me sayin'. Landlords receive enough rent without tenants doin' their work. Kettle's boilin'.'

Impertinent as well as inexperienced thought Sharples. 'I gather there's still no sign of the missing girls,' he said as he heaped a good scoop of leaves into the pot before pouring the boiling water over them.

'D.I. Clayton's at the 'ospital now. 'E'll find 'em, don't you worry.'

'D.I. eh? Good.'

Davies nodded, took a pad and pencil from his inside pocket. 'Now, tell me what happened yesterday evening,' he said taking the offered cup and saucer from Sharples, 'thank you Sir.'

Once the statement had been taken and Davies prepared to leave, Sharples pointed to faint footprints, by the seating.

'The cleaners must've overlooked them – but I'm positive they belong to the missing children.'

Davies studied the prints, and drew a sketch.

'I see you've spotted the smaller size is handed down.'

''Anded down Sir?'

'Yes, see how you've drawn the ridges, the large sole has them going across, whereas, on the smaller size, they

49

only appear on the edges. I'm very impressed Detective Davies.'

''Ow old were the children?'

'The youngest no more than three, the older girl, I'd say about eight possibly nine.'

Davies wrote the ages by the footprints. 'And you say they had fair curly hair and blue eyes.' Oliver started to say something. 'Yes Sir,' Davies's patience wearing thin, 'I've put it down, the littl'un had really blue eyes.' He tucked the pencil inside the pad and placed it in his pocket. 'I'll arrange for a photographer to take a proper picture of the footprints.' he said collecting his overcoat from the counter's top. 'Thank you for the tea, I'll let myself out.'

CLEANERS WERE busy outside the entrance to the Lake Hotel and did not notice Clayton slip past the door they'd wedged-open. He approached the bar. The barmaid, mistaking him for an early customer, flung a tea towel over her shoulder and shooed him away.

'Sorry luv, but we don't open 'til eleven.'

'Good,' Clayton smiled, 'then you've time to help me.' He showed her his warrant and placed the wash ticket on the bar top. 'Tell me anything you can about the woman who uses the washhouse during these hours.'

Alice wiped her hands and picked up the ticket. 'What's she done?' placing the ticket back on the bar top, 'I know who you mean, but she doesn't look like a criminal.'

Relieved he'd found someone who knew the injured lady Clayton relaxed. 'Tell me what you know about her,' he caught the concern in Alice's eyes, 'I assure you, she's done nothing wrong,' he added.

Alice put a hand on her shapely hip, 'Not much t'tell really, keeps herself to herself, gets on with 'er washing. Goes 'ome without a wave goodbye, no "see ya next week" nothing. We think she's new to Gorton an' a bit snooty.'

'Snooty?'

'You know, doesn't muck in, doesn't 'elp fold each other's sheets, that sort of thing, prefers to struggle alone. We've given up offerin' 'elp and leave her to it.'

Clayton ran his fingers across his mouth. 'What kind of washing does she have? I mean a large family wash, men's clothes or children's, that kind of thing.'

'Oh no men's clothes – though she does 'ave double sheets, patched to glory mind. And little knickers, vests, white socks, I'd say she's got two little girls.' Alice's brow crossed with a frown, 'Avva'said something wrong?'

Clayton turned away, his colour drained.

She ran to direct him to the nearest lavatory and returned to the bar. Sensing he'd offloaded whatever lay undigested, she put a scoop of ice into a pint glass and filled it with water. She returned to the loo, handed the glass to him, and waited whilst he took a mouthful, rinsed and spat it out. He flushed the cistern.

She soaked the tea towel and wrung it out. 'Here,' she said passing it to him, 'wipe the sweat off your face.'

He handed her the pint glass, leaned over the bowl and swilled his face with cold water. 'I'm so sorry,' he muttered running the damp cloth across his forehead.

'Don't worry,' Alice said as she handed him the glass. He took another mouthful, held back his head and gargled. From her viewpoint, Alice studied the policeman's profile and took in his dark lashes lowered with embarrassment and his Adam's apple covered with dark stubble. 'It's something to do with the woman's children, isn't it?' He straightened and turned towards her. She stepped

51

close, removed a fleck of towel fluff off his collar and asked, 'What's happened to them?'

'We don't know. Can I use the telephone?'

Alice nodded, pointed to the phone behind the bar. 'You'll have to dial 0 then the number,' she gestured towards the ceiling, 'landlord's rules.'

Handing her the towel, he started to dial. Alice threw it into the laundry bin, picked up a fresh one and began polishing glasses.

'Thanks, but it wasn't necessary,' Clayton said. 'The Super's not in.' He turned to leave, spotted the sign on the wall and realised what he'd done. 'Shit,' he said, 'did I throw up in the ladies?'

'Don't give it another thought,' Alice assured him, 'the cleaners 'ave worse after Saturday night.' She stopped polishing the glass she held. 'The woman, I didn't want you to think I don't like 'er. I feel a bit sorry for 'er – you know. Everything about 'er says she's struggling to keep body and soul together. Like she's got pride and lets it stop 'er making friends.' Clayton nodded.

'We're trying to piece what we can about her. She was knocked down yesterday, and has nothing to identify her except this wash ticket. It's all I've got to work on.' He turned again to leave. 'Thank you Alice and again I'm sorry about…' He gave a sideways nod towards the ladies toilet. 'Canteen food – not fit for pigs.'

She smiled and said she understood, continued polishing glasses and watched him walk out of the pub to head in the direction of the city.

'I'VE BEEN ringing your office all morning,' Wilson told Hammond, 'when I saw the visitors from Head Office, I thought they were onto you so kept away. I see you got my note. It took a bit of a risk, with Minshull Street's officers swarming around the car park.' He concealed a smile when alarm rose in Hammond's eyes. 'What did they want?' he asked.

'Oh some bloody silk complained to Henderson about rudeness amongst some of our officers and they roped us in – gave us all a bollicking.' Hammond spoke as though in a dream, his mind elsewhere.

'I got knocked out cold last night – all in the cause of your dirty business.'

'You? Knocked out?' Hammond gave Wilson a look of incredulity. 'Sure it wasn't Jenkins up to his old tricks?'

'Very funny,' Wilson didn't like to be reminded of the time when Jenkins split open his skull. 'Your Greek seaman seems to think he's paid you to protect his family. How does that fit with your other paymasters?'

They were stood on a bandstand in the middle of a deserted park, yet Hammond's frozen glare told Wilson he'd hit a nerve. He watched the Superintendent's eyes as they flitted around the park and back to face him.

'You have to understand, I know the Boss brothers are pressing me, but that's nothing I can't handle – the problem's closer to home.'

'Closer to home, you mean in the force?' Hammond didn't answer, he didn't have to: Wilson understood where the Super's fear lay. Years ago, Hammond could swing anything. He swung Wilson's injury declaring him fit for work when he wasn't – afterwards he had him transferred to Yorkshire. 'Is it the fella from the C.P.A.?'

Hammond nodded. 'Stupid sod was filmed having it off with his boyfriend.' He plunged his hands deep into his pocket. 'Now Alfredo's threatening to expose him if he goes down.'

'Nice fellas you hang out with.' Wilson couldn't give tuppence for any of them. He fingered the packet tucked inside his coat, smiled cruelly at Hammond's fraught expression and pulled out instead, his pack of cigarettes. 'So you don't want to see the Greek's message?' He clicked the Ronson and held the flame to the cigarette's tip. Hammond walked to the middle of the bandstand and came back thumping his fist on the balustrade. Droplets fell onto the deck splashing his highly polished shoes.

'This bloody barrister's going to make matters worse.   Because of him, I've got the Chief Constable snooping around – I'm bloody trapped. My department had nothing to do with the bloody car crash. It was Jenkins and Johnson's fuck up, nothing to do with me.'

'You mean last night's accident on London Road?'

'Yeh, some stupid woman got knocked down, the lads got her safely to hospital, cleared the site and got the traffic moving. Now, it seems she had two kids with her. They've disappeared – no one recalls seeing them, except the creep who's caused all this fuss.'

'The doll mender.'

'Yeh, well he owns the building near to where the accident took place – says they were in his shop minutes before being abducted.' Wilson bristled, watched Hammond plunge his hands into his pockets and walk into the middle of the bandstand once more. 'If only,' Hammond continued, unaware that Wilson hung onto his every word, 'bloody Johnson had shown some sense, took the creep's statement and showed him some respect – he wouldn't have gone blabbing to the silk.' He returned to Wilson's side.

'Did you say abducted?'

'Yeh, well that's what it looks like, bloody hell Mike – you know more than anyone how many perverts roam the streets.'

54

'Put me on the case.'

Hammond shot a glance at Wilson. 'No, I need you elsewhere.'

'But I'll solve it quickly, the eyes of Head Office will turn to other matters and you'll be left alone.'

'The court case is too close. I can't be sidetracked because a couple of nippers have gone missing.'

'But you've no choice; you said the Chief Constable will be watching Lever Street's every move until the case is solved.'

Hammond gave the park another sweeping glance. 'You might have a point,' he gave a shrug, 'if anyone can snoop out child abductors, you can – I've Clayton sniffing around at the moment, but he's a wasted space. Did you two ever meet?'

Wilson shook his head, wasn't interested in other employees of the force. 'I'd rather start my own line of enquiries but I'll need your backing if I have to pounce.'

Hammond rolled his eyes. 'None of your old tricks, do you hear me, make sure you've got solid evidence before you *pounce*. You'll need help, take Johnson and Jenkins, I'll square it with Benson – he owes me.' Hammond saw Wilson's reluctance, 'I know, but you'll need help and they were on the scene, besides you were mates once. I don't want any effing around, keep your fists to yourself and with luck, the kids'll be fine.'

'They'd better be.'

CHAPTER FOUR

AROUND MID morning, the plumber called at Lincoln House, received no reply from the flat above the Doll's Hospital and left a card requesting the tenant to contact the letting agent.

Oliver continued to repair dolls and puppets until his work was interrupted by a telephone call. It was William Gould.

'Would you care to join me for a drink in the Waldorf this evening, say 5.30, there's someone I'd like you to meet.'

Oliver readily agreed, he hadn't been invited to a pub since Elizabeth's death. Perhaps it was time to socialise once more. He returned to his workbench, the finished marionettes lay ready for packing. Wrapping each in tissue he mused how wonderful it would be if humans could be re-strung and polished with renewed vitality. Above him, something was being dragged across the floor, *at last*, he thought, the plumber had arrived to fix the leak.

CLAYTON TOOK the bus tickets out of his pocket and entered the depot's reception office. After introducing himself to the lady behind the desk, he passed the tickets to her. The injured woman's wet coat pocket had rubbed away some of the print but he hoped most of the information was still visible. She ironed them flat using the varnished nails of her index fingers.

'I'm sorry,' he said, 'they've been somewhere damp.'

She looked up at him and smiled. 'Not difficult in this weather, we're all damp, but not to worry, I can see the serial numbers well enough.' She crosschecked them against a row of figures in her ledger, the polished red pointer of her fingertip moving down the columns.

'Yes,' she said at last, 'Jimmy Aitkin's bus,' she closed the book and looked up, 'number 109.'

'If a person got on the bus from say, London Road Railway Station with these tickets, where would she alight?'

'That's easy Inspector,' she pulled a chart from a table behind the desk. 'It's a penny for every six stops, which takes your lady to…,' fascinated by the red nail Clayton watched it move along the bus route, '…here.' She turned the map around for him to make notes.

'Thanks, tell me, are both tickets for the 109?'

'Yes, one adult, one child issued by Jimmy yesterday.' She saw his face drop, 'is there something wrong Inspector?'

'It's just the information I have is the lady was travelling with *two* children.'

'Well she could be, the blue ticket is for a child aged between five and fourteen. She could have had another child under the age of five.' His face lit up revealing his dimples when he smiled. 'You should smile more often Inspector, it suits you.'

He thanked her and made to leave.

'Would you like to know where Jimmy's bus is at the moment Inspector?' She asked pulling another ledger onto the desk, 'maybe you could have a word with him.' She glanced up at the clock, 'he'll be passing here in fifteen minutes. Would you like a cup of tea?'

SMACK ON time the 109 rumbled to a halt outside the depot. Clayton jumped onto the platform and waited whilst the bus headed towards the city centre and the conductor collected his fares. After introducing himself, Clayton asked whether he remembered a female passenger travelling with two little girls.

'Why d'yer ask? Is summat wrong?'

'If you can recall, she wore a grey tweed coat.'

'And a little black hat.'

'Yes.' Clayton agreed, his mind returning to the hospital and the Matron's attempt to plump up the tiny feathers. 'It's her children we need descriptions of. Can you help?'

'If she's the one I'm thinking of, both have fair curly hair and big blue eyes. Good as gold they are.'

'Good, now I don't suppose you know where about on Clewes Street she lived?'

An elderly passenger got up from her seat. Aitkin rang the bell and held out a hand to steady her passage. At the stop he assisted her off the platform, gave the bell a couple of rings and came back to Clayton. He lowered his voice, 'Who said she lived on Clewes Street?'

'The depot – said that was where the ticket took her.'

'Look,' Jimmy said keeping his voice low, 'I don't want trouble with the depot, but I didn't charge 'er full price.'

'So you know where she lives?'

'No, I don't,' the conductor shrugged his shoulders, 'but I think it must be somewhere near to Peacock's works.'

'Peacock's the locomotive factory?' Clayton's expression showed disbelief.

'I know,' said the conductor, sharing his thoughts, 'bugger all there except railway sidings and the red rec.'

CLAYTON CARRIED a hot cup of tea across the office just as Davies walked in. He gave it to his rain-soaked junior and set to making another.

'How did you get on with the statements?'

'Oh most said the same thing – police officers too rude by far. But cuttin' to the nitty gritty Sir, there seem to be a few things we could look at.' He took a sip of his tea. 'Yuk - there's no sugar in it.'

Clayton rolled his eyes, took the cup back to the sink and heaped sugar in whilst Davies continued.

'I've split the pedestrians up – depending on which side of the road they stood. Those who crossed from the railway side; saw the woman but didn't see any children. They noticed she was in a hurry and was already on the road before the traffic stopped.'

'Did uniform get any of this last night?' Clayton carried two steaming mugs and placed them onto the desk.

'Thanks Sir,' Davies gave his a blow before slurping a gulp. 'That's better,' he sighed.

'We aim to please.'

'If you ask me Sir, uniform's statements don't account for much. I've re-questioned those witnesses in Johnson's report, thought we might compare.'

'Good lad - go on – give me the rest of the nitty gritty.'

Davies took another slurp. 'The pedestrians crossing the road from the same side as the woman say they couldn't see much of the woman because a man in a dark coat ran between her and them blocking their view. None noticed any children but most saw a tramp rummaging through the litter bin.'

'Amazing the things people get upset by.'

'Yeh,' Davies gave his tea another loud slurp.

'Yes, did you find any more about the man in the dark coat?'

'Seemed t'be in two places at one time. Early pedestrians saw 'im arguing with a merchant seaman. Others saw 'im on the other side of the road. Black raincoats are ten a penny – could be two fellas.'

'Still, he could have taken the children, getting to the nitty gritty, he got pretty close to the woman.'

'Yeh, that's what I thought,' Davies put the statements to one side and opened another file; 'maybe he was with the woman.'

'Then why hasn't he turned up at the hospital?'

'Maybe 'e's got a wife an' those nippers are 'is. Y'know – daren't come forward in case the missus finds out.'

'Maybe.' Davies's logic was reasonable. 'Did you speak to any of the office workers along the terrace?' Clayton pointed to their sketched map.

'Yeh,' Davies turned the pages of the file ready, just as Constable Brown entered the office. His solemn face showed he was the bearer of bad news.

''Ad a phone call from the Infirmary Sir, last night's traffic victim died just after noon. The Matron said she didn't regain consciousness.'

Clayton gave a slow nod. 'Thank you Brown.'

'Sir?' Brown said as he turned to leave but had second thoughts, 'sorry no, it doesn't matter.' He left the room closing the door behind.

'So the driver will be charged with manslaughter eh?' Davies conjectured warming his hands on the hot mug.

Clayton wiped his hand over his mouth. 'Perhaps, or reckless driving, I've the feeling uniform couldn't care less what happens to her right now.'

'I always know you're onto summat when you do that.' Davies observed.

'Do what?'

'Wipe yer 'and across yer mouth.'

'Oh I wish it were true.' Clayton studied the sketch of the traffic lights and the surrounding buildings. 'If this man did take the children, where would he disappear to in such a short time? How far did you get with interviewing the business owners?'

'I started with the man who mends toys. He's given me a description of the children.'

'Good, then we can compare it with my bus conductor who…,' Clayton checked his watch, 'should be calling at the front desk any moment.' The phone rang, Clayton answered.

Davies pulled out Sharples's statement and passed it across the desk, the sketch of the footprints clipped to it.

Clayton replaced the receiver. 'The Evening News reporter's here, I want him to put the descriptions in the early edition.' He drained his tea and pointed to the sketch, 'Where did you get these?'

'From the man who mends toys: he says they belong to the missing children, I've ordered the photographer to take some pics.'

'Good lad,' Clayton picked Sharples's description and left to meet the bus conductor and newsman.

BOTH DESCRIPTIONS matched – the reporter left to give maximum coverage in the evening paper and when Clayton returned to the office, Davies had sifted through all the statements given.

'You mention somewhere,' said Clayton, 'the woman's bag was found under one of the vehicles at the scene of the accident, where is it?'

'Dunno Sir, but according to Mr Sharples, it's just an old shopping bag, not an 'andbag or owt.'

'But that's not the point, we need every scrap of information,' he threw his pen onto the desk, 'd'you get the feeling uniform aren't up to scratch Davies?'

'Always Sir.'

'I want you to continue questioning the office workers and residents along that terrace on London Road; show them the sketches, jog their memories. Someone's got to remember something.' He slid the street map into his inside pocket. 'I'm off to knock on a few doors myself, the bus conductor thinks the woman lived somewhere near Gorton Tank.'

Davies looked up from his files. 'Aren't many doors to knock on around Gorton Tank Sir.'

'So I believe. But why do I get the feeling it could be a long night?'

OLIVER SHARPLES bade his customer farewell, closed the drawer to his till and returned to the back room. A shout from the hall caused him to turn back and catch a glimpse of the man apologizing for not closing the outer door.

'You really have them puzzled Albert,' he said stepping into the main hall. 'They wonder where the voice comes from.'

'I don't care. What does it take to make sure the bloody door closes properly?'

'If you're wondering what's happening upstairs,' Oliver said, looking into the black space behind the staircase, 'I've reported a leak in flat four. Please Albert – I beg you, don't give the plumber a bad time.'

'E's bin and gone – didn't get any reply.'

'Oh? It's just I thought I heard…never mind.' Oliver turned to go, 'I have to get back to work.'

Albert shuffled in the darkness. 'Yeh Oliver I know – but the shifty bloke – the one in flat four, a'think 'e's flitted.'

'Oh? The agent didn't say.'

'Good riddance – I say.'

'Yes well – you never did like him. But look, sorry Albert, I must get back to my work.'

'Yeh – I know.'

Oliver re-entered his shop and resumed repairing toys. The residents of Lincoln House and their petty squabbles were none of his business. He merely owned the block; it was the agent's job to vet the tenants. He looked up at the stain – it had dried but left a mark – unease crept into his psyche. What if the tenant had a dog or something?

A FEW ancient gas lamps gave off a dim glow – Clayton pulled his collar around his ears and headed for a pub tucked in the hollow by the railway embankment. It was a dreary place, tobacco-yellowed walls and a flameless smoky fire. Mistaking him for an early customer, a portly woman greeted Clayton with a painted smile as he entered the ill-named snug. The smile faded when he introduced himself and asked if she recognised the faces sketched by the station's artist.

'No,' she shook her head, 'no families live 'ere any more, 'ouses were flattened durin' the war.' She inclined her head to the rear of the pub, 'Bombs were aimed at Peacocks and Gorton Tank but took me bloody customers' 'omes instead.' She lit a cigarette, 'Now I'm left scratching a livin' on shift workers an' such.'

With every finger covered in diamond rings, Clayton was not impressed with the landlady's plea of poverty. The barman gave the sketches a quick glance, shook his head and continued cleaning the beer pumps.

Glad to be out again, Clayton stood with his back to Peacock's wall and stared across the deserted open space known locally as red rec. Dots of light glowed in the distance, he headed for them and the sound of machines whined through the murky air as he neared the double gates of a small factory. He banged to gain admittance but couldn't make himself heard. Pushing the gate against the lock he peered through the chink – a van was parked in front of what appeared to be the main entrance. He rattled the gate calling to catch the attention of someone and scanned the surrounding area – the nearest light coming from a chip shop and beyond that, the orange glow of electric street lamps. Silhouetted against this the outline of distant rooftops brought a droplet of cheer. He ran towards the light, the smell of freshly cooked food causing his stomach to roll and ordered fish and chips. When the fryer coated both sides of the filleted hake and dropped it to sizzle in the scalding fat, Clayton showed the sketches of the dead woman and her girls. The man wiped his hands, took the pictures to the one light hanging from the ceiling and nodded.

'She'll pass my shop tomorrow evening. On 'er way to do 'er washin', but the kids I've not seen.' He passed the sketches back to Clayton, returned to his cooking range and rolled back the cover where pale sticks of potato bubbled noisily. He lifted the basket, gave the chips a shake and lowered it to hiss and froth.

'D'y'know where she lives?' Clayton shouted above the sizzling.

The fryer shook his head, rolled the range lid down and opened the one containing the fish. Clayton was reminded of the stainless steel washing machines used in the public washhouse. His stomach rolled again as he watched his meal materialise in front of him, sprinkled with salt and vinegar and presented on sheets of freshly torn newspaper.

'No, dunno where she lives,' the fryer continued as he handed over the packaged food, 'but I think she works in Whitelady's the sewing factory.' Clayton turned around to view the dimly lit building set in the middle of nowhere. 'The gates'll open in ten minutes; but be quick mind, they don't stay open long.'

Clayton made it back to the factory, newspaper scorching the palms of his hands. The machines still humming steadily – he leaned against the fence and devoured chips – too hot to handle – but delicious. Light arched across the crushed brick ground as a gap opened in the gate and shadows of people scuttered in different directions. Hastily, Clayton re-wrapped his meal and stowed it into the huge pocket inside his raincoat. He fought against the tide of workers until he reached the opening and managed to place his boot in the gap just as the gate closed.

'Hang on,' he shouted, as metal tightened against his foot. It slackened and a man in shirtsleeves and lightweight trousers came into view. His gold watch glistened against the exterior light making Clayton assume he was the manager at least. He pressed his warrant towards the man's face, 'D.I. Clayton from Lever Street Police Station. I want a word about an employee of yours.'

The man gave Clayton a wave of dismissal, 'It's very late Inspector, can't it wait until the morning?'

'No it can't,' Clayton retorted. 'If you want visitors to make appointments, get a decent reception desk.' The gate opened, the white shirted man gave a sigh and allowed Clayton to slide through before closing it again. He slipped the padlock into the lock and clicked it shut. He nodded towards the entrance and gestured for Clayton to follow.

HIS NERVES on edge and leaks in ceilings – Oliver had had enough. He'd tried to concentrate on his work – but new noises coming from the flat were driving him mad. Either the plumber had attained access after all, or the tenant was moving out. But he decided he'd break the golden rule and confront whoever was there, once and for all.

Albert's silent gait and sightless gaze caught him unawares on the staircase.

'That you Oliver?'

'Yes Albert, what're you doing up here?'

''Eared a bang, went to see what 'e's up to.'

'Yes, that's all very well, but he's nothing to do with you, come on and let me help you down.'

'I can manage well enough, it's 'im needs lookin' after. 'E's not right y'know, don't *smell* right.'

Oliver let out a loud laugh, relaxing at last. 'Oh Albert, you can't go falling out with neighbours, just because you don't like their smell.'

Holding the rail with one hand Albert took the stairs as well as any sighted person. ''E's up to sommat, I know it.'

'Yes, well if he's moving out, you'll not have to worry about him any more, did the plumber come back?'

'Nah, but that young police detective's been askin' questions – an' the other fella.'

They reached the bottom and Albert turned toward his darkened room, where he sat unseen and unseeing day and night listening to the comings and goings of Lincoln House. Oliver plumped the cushions of his chair and guided him into it.

'Well I'm pleased to hear that the police are taking an interest.' Oliver relaxed again, glad someone was taking the missing children seriously at last, 'My nerves are that edgy, Albert, my mind's been thinking all sorts of things.'

'Yeh, well if it's owt to do wi'im upstairs – you'll not be far wrong.'

'I even thought he'd got a dog or something.' Oliver said as he turned to go.

'No dog, but he's up to summat – an' the smell up on that landin' – wot does 'e need to disinfect when he already stinks of carbolic anyway?'

Oliver shook his head, not in answer to Albert's question, merely to dispel the crazy prejudices the blind man held for certain people. Feeling much better, he returned to the Doll's Hospital, finished parcelling the repaired toys and locked up for the night.

CLAYTON SCANNED the factory floor, a few workers still remaining, some manning sewing machines, others pulling rails bearing coat hangers of clothes towards the entrance.

The manager stood with his back to the door, 'I can give you a few minutes Inspector, but I have a deadline to reach. These garments must be loaded, ready for shipment tonight.'

'Then the sooner my questions are answered to my satisfaction, Mr er..,' no name was offered, 'then the sooner you can return to your work. Is there somewhere we can talk without interruption?'

Again the man gave a loud sigh, pointed to a set of open tread steps and took the lead.

His office was dominated by a huge table littered with hand drawn sketches of models wearing evening dresses and sample swatches of the suggested materials, stapled to each design. All around the walls – the logo 'Whitelady modes' blazoned, and the only seat, a stool by the draughtsman's board – was offered to Clayton.

'Please, take a seat, I must have a word with my staff,' the manager turned towards the door, Clayton barred his exit. 'Look Inspector, I've a really tight deadline. This will take me just a couple of minutes.'

'My work has a deadline too and much more important than a few frocks on rails. So sit down and answer my questions.'

Irritated, the sewing factory manager sat on the table's corner, 'Some of my employees come from troubled parts of world, they…'

'Oh please, I'm not here on behalf of immigration, though of course,' he paused for effect, 'from time to time we *can* and *do* work together.' Clayton took the sketches from his inside pocket. 'My enquiries concern this lady and her children.'

Those machines that were still in operation on the work floor below stopped, and popular songs could be heard via the factory's tannoy system – music whilst they worked? *Fat chance*, thought Clayton *they'd never hear it*. The man sitting on the corner of the table stared at the sketches in his hand. He looked up, 'Is she alright?' he whispered.

'Who? Which *she* are we talking about?'

'The woman, Kathleen.'

'She was knocked down yesterday evening and at lunchtime today, died of her injuries.' Clayton watched the man's face, his olive complexion paled tones of grey. He cared for this employee, he could see. 'The children she had with her were taken from the scene. We're trying to pick up their trail.'

A woman's voice called from the workshop below the office, the manager turned to listen, nodded his consent and faced Clayton, his deadline taking second place in his thoughts.

'It's what she always dreaded, I can't believe…,' he stared at the faces held in his hands, like theirs; his features drawn, 'she was always so careful.' Tears moistened his eyes, 'You say you're picking up their trail, you mean something has happened to Audrey and Linda?'

Clayton nodded, 'They're missing.'

'Missing?' Suspicion entered the sad eyes, sharpening his features. 'Who are you really?' he asked.

'I've already told you,' Clayton answered taken aback by the difference in the manager's attitude, his hostility having nothing to do with the delay of his shipment.

'You've been sent by *him* haven't you? Where did you say you were from? I should have known – does the corrupt Sergeant Hammond still operate from there?'

Clayton's mind raced, *corrupt Sergeant Hammond?* He stared at the man in front of him. To call the Super corrupt was dangerous indeed, to refer to Hammond as a *Sergeant*, was suicidal. 'I work under my own direction, nobody sent me here. And yes, Superintendent Hammond is at Lever Street.'

'Oh, so it's Superintendent now is it?' He scrunched the sketches in his hands and stood up. 'That can only mean there are others just as corrupt higher in the ranks.' He stopped inches from Clayton, his nerve rising with his temper.

'I think you'd better sit down Mr er, you never did tell me your name.'

Not listening to anything Clayton said, the manager shook his head trying to make sense of something. Eventually he reasoned, 'She's not dead – is she? He's caught up with her and she's fled again.' The sketches had formed a compact ball in his hands, he flung it across the office, bouncing off the drawing board and landing in the wastepaper bin. 'Get out,' he yelled into Clayton's face. Below employees stopped their work and looked up concern for their boss on their faces.

Clayton stooped to pick the sketches out of the bin. He unravelled the ball and spread out each drawing on top of the littered table. 'I wish you hadn't done that,' he said easing the creases out with his fingers. 'They're all I've got.' He turned to look at the manager, 'I got these descriptions from a bus conductor who directed me to this area.' He took the street map out of his pocket and the smell of fish and chips filled the air causing his stomach to roll.

'Your supper?'

The tension relaxed, Clayton laughed, 'Supper? Breakfast more like. I haven't eaten since the crap served to me first thing by the canteen. I threw it up, thank God. I don't know what trouble you've had with Superintendent Hammond, he's a law unto himself and I'm my own man. In fact, we do our best not to cross paths.'

The factory manager held out a hand, 'Whiteman, Otto Whiteman, or before I fled the Nazis – Weismann.'

Clayton took the offered hand. 'So, if you are to make your shipment and I'm to eat my *supper* I suggest you tell me what you know about the lady and her two children.'

'Yes, why not?' his manner brighter, 'Kathleen's employed as a cutter and I don't mind telling you, that in the rag trade, they're worth their weight in gold. She's the best there is and came to me highly recommended.' He turned to face the shop floor, gave his workers a nod and watched them resume their work. Light caught the chrome of the rails as they were pushed towards the entrance beneath the office. Whiteman sighed, 'Kathleen and the girls left Yorkshire where they lived in fear of her brutish husband – a man who cannot control his temper. That's why I was reluctant to give you her address – in case it got back to him.'

The hackles on Clayton's back sprung up, 'What kind of a bloke do you think I am?'

'A policeman kind of a bloke.'

'Oh, I see, yeh I forgot you have a phobia of coppers.'

Whiteman's mouth tightened – his lips thinned with renewed rage, 'No Detective Inspector, I don't have a phobia of police, though I've experienced the worse type there is, and so has Kathleen,' he paused; his breath fraught with anger, 'and also little Audrey.'

Clayton nodded, comprehension shaking the scales from his eyes. 'Kathleen's husband is a policeman. Yeh, I get it now. But didn't you say she was from Yorkshire?'

'Yes and she thought she'd shaken him off at last.' Whiteman appeared to have got his rage under control. 'My reluctance was caused by fear that he'd found her. You see before he and Kathleen met, he worked at Lever Street Police Station.' He glanced down at his employees. 'Anyway because of her fear, Kathleen couldn't settle anywhere too long. In fact she planned to move on last weekend.' He reached for a notepad and scribbled down an address. Tearing off the page, he handed it over, 'I don't know her new address but no doubt it will be somewhere cheap and cheerful. If it's any use to you, this is her old place.' He picked up his keys in readiness to escort Clayton off the premises. 'Sorry I can't help you more, but there it is.'

Unconvinced by the change of heart, Clayton ignored the written note. 'No Mr Whiteman, there it isn't. I want to see your books, those that contain the details of your employees. It might take some time, so relax and,' using the flat of his hand he indicated to the corner of the table, 'sit down.'

'But I've told you all I know.'

'You've told me the traffic victim is called Kathleen, her children are Audrey and Linda and they originate from Yorkshire where their father is a policeman with a bad temper. At this moment in time Kathleen lies on a mortuary slab and her girls have been abducted.' He let that sink in. 'Regardless of your objections to the force, we're their only hope. Now stop playing games and tell me where they lived.'

With a well-laundered handkerchief, Whiteman wiped the sweat from his face. He opened his safe and brought out a cash box. 'She wanted me to bank most of her wages.' He flicked a bankbook onto the table.

'This gives the factory as her address,' Clayton said opening it.

Whiteman held a miniature knitted gollywog into the air – three keys were tied to the ribbon around its neck. 'Audrey made this for me. She said as I wouldn't want it for Christmas, I could accept it as a Passover gift.' He took a deep breath, 'come Inspector, I'll take you to their home.'

OLIVER FOUND the Waldorf Hotel inviting and typical of the heart of city pubs he remembered from before the war. Gould waved from the corner of the room; Oliver waved back noting the thin man with wiry grey hair who sat by the barrister's side. Gould signalled for the waiter to attend their table and stood to greet the doll mender.

'Glad you could make it Mr Sharples, what's your poison?'

'Scotch: thank you, and please, my name's Oliver.'

Gould ordered the drinks and indicated to Oliver, the cloak stand nearby.

'I must say,' said Oliver, 'this is very civilised, especially in this weather.'

The waiter brought a tray of drinks, replaced the soda siphon and ashtray before leaving the men to their own company.

Gould turned the siphon for Oliver to use first. 'I'd like you to meet my friend Charlie Faulkner. In my opinion, he's the best private detective in the business. Charlie's helping us pick up the trail of the missing children.'

Oliver shook Faulkner's hand before settling down to enjoy the scotch and soda.

Gould continued, 'Charlie's been working on a case which involves Lever Street Police Station and some of its officers. He's particularly interested in the movements of Superintendent Hammond and associates, isn't that so Charlie?'

Oliver knew nothing of police station personnel only that the accident was being handled from there. 'What's this to do with the little girls?'

'Hopefully, it hasn't *anything* to do with them.' Faulkner said before opening his notebook. 'But it helps to know who you're working with.' He cleared his throat and began to read his report. 'I've spent today questioning people who live and work along London Road. In Lincoln House where your 'hospital' is located, the man who appears to know everything, informed me that unusual activity has occurred with the tenant from flat four.'

Oliver put down his glass. 'Oh, that's old Albert. He's blind; and thinks he sees what's going on when all he can do is detect a blast of cold air from the front door.' He could see his interruption irritated the private detective but thought it needed to be said. 'Albert's a dear old thing, but you mustn't allow his comments to blow you off course Mr Faulkner. He lives in a world of his own which, I'm afraid to say; is very prejudiced. He doesn't like the fellow in flat four.' He picked up his glass and took a gulp of whiskey, 'I'm fond of Albert but he can test the patience of a saint.'

Faulkner turned the page of his notebook. 'That might be the case, but there's nothing wrong with Albert's hearing. He's heard things moving in that flat when I know the tenant was at work and in full view of his workmates.'

'That must have been the plumber, I told Albert about the plumber.'

'Albert told me the noises you heard were nothing to do with the plumber. I checked with the letting agents, the plumber didn't get a reply.'

'I even thought Albert had knocked something over,' continued Oliver, 'he fumbles about in the dark scaring people half to death.' He looked across the table at Charlie's twitching moustache, 'I'm sorry Mr Faulkner – I shouldn't have interrupted you again. It's just that I've had a dreadful day with one thing and another, first it was the leak, then the noises.' He gave a feint laugh; 'finally I thought the damned tenant must have taken in a pet or something, a dog I thought…' the men sat opposite raised their eyebrows. 'Oh no…oh my goodness, you don't think? We must inform the police at once.'

CHAPTER FIVE

ACTING DETECTIVE Inspector Wilson was not looking forward to questioning the man he'd pulled in. He told Hammond he needed specialised help but the Super's only reply was to use whatever methods were available without resorting to violence. He paced the floor, the suspect watching his every move like a spectator at a tennis match. Wilson felt nervous – there was something about the man's eyes he didn't like, and his smell reminded him of hospitals.

'Detective Constable Davies Sir, the Super's sent me to give you an'and.'

'Yeh, what are you then, a bloody miracle worker? I didn't expect the fella to be deaf and dumb. How the hell am I goin' to interrogate him?'

Davies took a seat at the table and offered writing materials to the man opposite. It was all very irregular and nothing akin to the training given by Clayton.

'I feel I should tell you Sir, this man's supervisor says he was working at the time of the accident, so therefore…'

'I don't need you to tell me anything. Got it Davies?'

Davies did get it, within a few minutes of returning to his desk, he'd learned Wilson had authorised a full-scale search of the man's flat, the Parcel Depot where he worked and the guards' vans on each platform of London Road Railway Station. Police dogs were swarming over every parcel in the city's Post Offices and all the trains had come to a complete standstill. Davies studied the man across the table and found him easier to be with – than the agitated police officer pacing the floor behind.

'Okay, D.I. Wilson, David MacLean's confirmed 'is name and address. What d'yer want me to ask?'

'Where's he put the kids?'

Davies passed his question to MacLean and waited whilst he wrote his reply, Wilson's pacing made him nervous. He glanced at his watch, wishing Clayton would arrive and take over.

''E says what kids?'

Wilson flew past Davies's right side and grabbed the lapels of MacLean's brown overall, catching the man's bottom lip with his signet ring.

'Don't play the innocent with me sunshine,' he spat through gritted teeth as the suspect's blood ran onto Wilson's hand. Davies shot from his chair, grabbed Wilson's shoulder and pulled him off MacLean. He could feel the rage running though Wilson's body.

'Leave 'im Sir, that's not the way.'

Wilson threw Davies off: spun round and was about to lash out. 'Don't ever try to tell me how to handle perverts.' He shrunk back, shot a glance at MacLean and resumed his pacing.

MacLean sat swabbing the cut lip with his handkerchief, his eyes moving from one side of his head to the other – watching Wilson's every move. Davies wrote asking if he was okay, MacLean nodded briefly then returned his attention to the man behind Davies's back.

'D.I. Clayton'll be back soon Sir, maybe we should wait for 'im.'

'Ha,' the laugh had no humour, 'not from what I've heard Davies, I hear the man plods around in circles.'

'No Sir, you 'eard wrong D.I. Clayton asks questions and gets results.'

'So where was he when we caught sunshine here?'

'E's following information which might lead to the woman's 'ome.'

'Oh yeh and where would that be?' Wilson stopped pacing and moved nearer to Davies eager to know what Clayton had discovered.

'Dunno Sir, somewhere near Peacocks works on the 109 route.'

Wilson stepped back and sneered, 'Yeh, well what's keepin' him. There's bugger all there.'

Davies nodded, 'Yeh, that's what he said.'

'In the meantime, we've got sunshine here with us,' he raised a clenched fist at MacLean, 'and one way or another; he's goin' to tell us where he's hidden the kids.' He caught the look on Davies's face, lowered his arm and resumed his pacing. 'His eyes, Davies, look at his eyes – do they give you the shits?'

'No Sir, why?'

'Nothing.' Wilson avoided MacLean's gaze, stared instead at the ring on his finger and continued to pace the floor. He shouldn't have gone for him, not so early in the questioning but he'd spent all afternoon doing exactly what he'd accused Clayton of – plodding around in bloody circles. Sheer luck came his way when the doll mender arrived at the front desk just as Wilson walked into the building. Hammond gave him full rein to pull the bastard in and find the girls. He gave the ring a turn, blood oozed from beneath it, sticky where flesh met metal. The uniformed officer guarding the door looked impassive – his gaze fixed towards the window.

Hutton shared his views when it came to perverts, he'd told him as much.

'Look,' Wilson told Davies, 'I can't work like this - it's driving me mad. He's got the kids hidden somewhere. And writing little notes back and forth isn't going to find them. If anyone needs to know where I am, tell 'em I've gone to see if the traffic victim has regained consciousness.'

Davies looked up from his notepad. 'But Sir, didn't you know? The woman…'

'She's not your concern Davies.' Wilson snapped grabbing his jacket from the vacant chair beside Davies. 'Get what you can from him, and I don't give a fuck how.' He stormed off leaving the door open wide.

Davies let out an audible sigh. He turned to Hutton, ''asn't anyone told 'im the woman's dead?' Hutton gave a shrug and closed the door. Davies thought he saw concern in MacLean's face and wondered fleetingly, whether he'd read his lips. Pulling his chair close, he wrote on the pad asking if MacLean knew the children's mother had died. The man held his handkerchief to his bloody lip and shook his head. D.C Davies hadn't got it wrong – there was a definite tinge of sadness in those piercing blue eyes.

CLAYTON FOLLOWED Whiteman down the stairs and onto the shop floor. 'Please wait here Inspector – I must speak to my workers. The van has to be loaded on time.'

He gave his consent and watched Whiteman check the lines of clothes hung on chrome rails. Two men and a woman listened to his instructions, nodding at intervals. Once satisfied that the loading could progress without his supervision, Whiteman returned to Clayton and led him to a locked storeroom. Shelves filled with rolls of materials lined the walls, together with boxes of thread, zips and buttons. Hidden in a corner was a door and using one of the keys on the gollywog's ribbon – he opened it.

Inside, the room gave the feeling of more space than was there. The windows, like those of the factory were set high up the walls. Light could pour through yet privacy maintained. An electric fire with timber surround made a cosy corner; either side of it were two velvet chairs. Clayton picked up knitting which rested on the arm of one.

'That's probably Audrey's work. She's always making things.' Whiteman pointed to the dining table and the stack of sample books. 'She uses all my colour swatches to make clothes for that doll of theirs.'

Clayton glanced around the room. 'Does Kathleen live here alone?'

Whiteman knew to what the detective alluded. 'Yes, quite definitely; she lived here in safety with her girls. I can assure you my friendship with her was purely platonic as well as a good business arrangement.'

'The bedrooms?' Whiteman nodded to where Clayton pointed, stood back whilst the detective examined each room. The furniture was sparse but of good quality, the double bed made ready with sheets turned back. He opened the wardrobe; two cotton dresses hung from the rail. Other clothing was stacked neatly on the shelves. The second room was furnished in a similar manner, except for a huge golliwog resting on the pillows in the centre of the double bed.

'He belongs to Audrey but like the doll, he's shared. Poor Kathleen has repaired him so many times, he's more thread than original material.' Whiteman shook his head, 'Unnecessary damage caused by her husband's bouts of rage.' He plunged his hands deep into his pockets. 'You come in contact with all kinds of humanity Inspector, what makes a man treat his family in such a manner?'

'I'm not sure I'd like to know,' Clayton glanced at the toy propped up against the pillows. 'It must be some kind of illness.' He strolled back to the large living room. 'Did Kathleen have a handbag? We found only a purse and what she stood in.'

The clothes manufacturer gave Clayton a sad smile. 'I know,' he said, 'that huge purse with barely a couple of coppers in. She's never had a handbag as long as I've known her. You know she's had to cut her losses so many times – she's probably left it behind somewhere.'

'Are there any photographs of the children?'

'When I picked her up from the railway station, apart from the pram which contained the toys and Linda, they owned what they stood in.'

'Where's the pram kept?'

Clayton followed Whiteman down a quarry-tiled passage; to the left was a W.C on the right, a door to a garage. It was empty except for the pram. Clayton peered inside, gave a nod and pointed to a side door.

'It leads onto the recreational ground. Kathleen used this to come and go.'

'It's like a fortress,' Clayton whispered, 'where did the girls play?'

'I had this converted for my purposes, Inspector – not to house children.'

It was reasonable Clayton granted. 'I can see why it should appeal to someone living in fear.'

'It does and I did.' Whiteman held Clayton's stare. 'Have you seen enough? My shipment is urgent.'

The ticking over of the van's engine informed Whiteman his employees had completed the loading. He opened the gates and fastened them back. Clayton strolled through, crushed brick crunching under his boots – hands deep in pockets and thoughts mulling deeper.

'Can I give you lift into town?' Whiteman offered. 'It isn't out of my way.'

Clayton beamed a smile and nodded.

Whiteman warmed to the detective and laughed as he put on his jacket, left final instructions to his employees and climbed into the cab.

'My wife often tells me,' he said as he drove through the gates, 'if she's ever going to leave me. It would be for a jazz musician with dimples.' He returned the wave of the worker manning the gates and headed for the road, 'You don't play a saxophone do you?'

DIVERTED TRAFFIC caused by the searches of the Railway Station, Post Office and Parcel Depot made journeying through the city slow. Not in the mood to wait, Wilson turned off the main drag and wove through the labyrinth of side streets. He needed to get across town, needed to take a closer look at the woman, needed to know if she was indeed Kathleen, pain griped his lower abdomen. Bloody hospitals.

Extra buses put on to disperse passengers unable to use the rail services did nothing to ease the congestion. Wilson found he was trapped in a standstill and couldn't re-join the main road; he pulled into a pub car park, bought a pack of cigarettes and used their toilet. His head was spinning; visions of mutilated kids stuffed behind bath panels or under floorboards haunted him together with MacLean's horrible eyes. Shelving the hospital visit, he drove out of the car park and backtracked towards London Road pulling up at the rear of Lincoln House.

Thoughts sped through Wilson's mind at breakneck speed. The doll mender, he recalled, had reported stains to the ceiling of his workshop, but searches revealed nothing gruesome. Yet the flat above had been thoroughly cleansed – why? He left the car and walked towards the less dim lights of London Road. Across the road, police vehicles – dog handlers mainly – lined the entrance to the Parcel Depot where MacLean had been employed for twenty years.

Wilson gave a brief nod to the policeman guarding the doorway to Lincoln House. He passed the Doll's Hospital and climbed the stairs. Pausing at flat four's door, he took a deep breath and pushed it open. Streetlight lit the room and fell on the splintered and cracked floorboards propped against the walls. He stepped inside treading gingerly, the gaps made by removed floorboards transformed to black ruts across the floor. Before him the bathroom door stood ajar; inside cupboards and panelling stripped bare, and a pile of debris stacked in a heap by the doorway. As he turned to leave; something skittered aside his boot and fell into a hole – dust softening its land.

'Oose that?' Gravel like and demanding, the voice made Wilson jump. He swung towards the door; the light of the landing's single bulb falling directly onto Albert's scarred and eyeless face.

'Christ! Where did you come from?'

'Sorry, thought it was 'im come back from prison.' Albert's horrific features moved from the glare as he returned to the stairs.

Wilson's heart settled to its normal manic rhythm. Christ – he thought – first a dumb man's eyes give the shits now a blind man's voice. He stepped over the ripped up floorboards and onto the landing. Albert was halfway down the stairs his feet taking the steps as well as any sighted person. Wilson watched him go, closed the door of flat four behind him and followed. In the dust beneath the floorboards a hair slide fashioned in the shape of a capital 'A' lay hidden from view.

82

CHAPTER SIX

TRAFFIC: MORE than was usual headed towards them. Whiteman cursed; his cleared exit barred by policemen manning the junctions.

'What the hell's going on?'

Clayton shook his head. 'You were saying about Kathleen's family?'

Whiteman pulled the handbrake and sat back. 'She didn't say much; only that her father died some years back and she kept in touch with her mother via the pub she frequented. Her mother's sister tried to keep friendly though, arranged a family reunion once. Audrey mentioned meeting her Nanna but said she wasn't nice and had no patience.' The traffic moved on Whiteman inched forward five or six car lengths then was stopped again by the policeman up ahead. He cursed in German.

Keeping him focused on the missing children Clayton asked, 'You mentioned something about Kathleen needing an address?'

'Yes, she toyed with writing to a relative she'd met at the party, but didn't want to disclose where she lived. I said she could use my home address. Thank God for that, now we can move on.' He gave the policeman another curse and crossed the junction. Ahead the road was clear but in the distance a cluster of brake lights reflecting on the wet road told him another delay was ahead.

'And did she?'

'Did she what?

'Write to this relative?'

'Don't think so, well if she did, they've not replied. Obviously, if anything arrives I'll let you know. But don't expect me to enter your police station.'

Clayton took out his notepad. 'I'll give you my secret address, used only by my informants. My desk phone number – only myself and Davies my D.C. answer it.' The van lurched to a sharp stop when the car in front broke fiercely. 'Look,' said Clayton handing the slip of paper to Whiteman, 'drop me off here, you can divert at this next left. Avoid the city altogether. I'll let you know in advance if I need another visit to the flat.'

He watched the van as it sped off to meet Whiteman's precious shipment, the dress manufacturer's words going over in his mind; like the Super's involvement with racketeers, gangsters and bent lawyers. And Whiteman's warning that others, higher in the ranks stood ready to protect Hammond. Clayton's closest friend, Barry Brocklehurst knew Hammond during those early days – when he returned to the station, he'd sound him out. Meanwhile, he pulled the fish and chips from the deep pocket in his raincoat and opened up the newspaper. Chips gone soggy but inside the batter, the fish was hot and tasty.

As he walked and munched, he tried to fathom who else in Lever Street was corrupt, Benson? Highly likely, but not Parker – too idle to be bent, anyway D.I. Parker dealt with vice – helps to be twisted when dealing with vice. The rain eased off and the temperature dropped. Traffic leaving the city was easing. So it should, thought Clayton checking the time on his watch, the rush hour ended ages ago. Having eaten all the fish, he scrunched the remaining food inside the newspaper and dropped it into the nearest bin.

Allowing the pavement to relax his mind, he meandered along, crossed at the lights and headed for Oxford Road where he hoped to catch Joe, his informant, and share a couple of pints. Haze haloed the streetlamps as the night air lowered in temperature and when he turned direction, needle sharp breezes pierced Clayton's face. He breathed in, inhaling the cold city air enjoying its iciness cleansing his lungs. If what Whiteman had said about Hammond was true – then during the war, he'd turned a blind eye to extortion, arson and murder – worse than turning a blind eye, he'd been implicit in destroying vital evidence? How was Clayton going to report Kathleen's address and whom could he trust? What if Hammond recognised Whiteman from the past?

The pub where he met Joe was empty. The unhappy landlord reading the racing pages of the sport's section didn't even bother to greet his sole customer.

'Joe been in?'

'Not yet Ian, bitter?'

'Aye,' he placed the correct change on the bar, picked up the news part of the landlord's paper and took a seat by the fire. The journalist had made a good job of attracting the public's attention. Clayton looked at the sketches and the captions beneath each one. He knew their names now, and where they lived. The plea for anyone who recognised the children to come forward was useless. Their home was a prison, no school, no doctor, and no one except their mother and Otto Whiteman ever saw them.

He stared at Audrey's face, highly intelligent according to Whiteman, sharper than the average eight year old, a girl who patiently taught her sister to read. Clayton nodded his thanks as the pint was placed on the table – he took a long drink – it went down well. Next, his attention went to Kathleen. The artist had picked up the lines of worry and etched them over her once, handsome face. Then there was the sketch of little Linda, three years old and a picture of perfect innocence.

'Wot yer doin' 'ere?' the familiar voice enquired over the top of the newspaper, 'thought yer'd be swankin' up at yer station?'

'Swanking? What've I got to swank about?' He folded the paper and took it back to the bar: the landlord already pulling Joe's pint.

''Bout catchin' the fella wot killed them kids.'

'Killed,' despite the beer quenching his thirst, Clayton's mouth ran dry, 'how?'

'Yer don't know? All of Manchester's been snarled up fer hours. Bloody 'ell Ian – where've yer been?'

The landlord brought two pints to the table; Clayton stood up and paid for both. He pushed his arm through the sleeve of his coat. 'I've been on a case, tell me what's happened, and make it quick, I shouldn't be here.'

'Sit down lad, there's nowt yer can do for'em. Pervert got 'em.'

The supper lying in Clayton's stomach stopped digesting. As an experienced copper he'd seen plenty of gory crimes, but had never hardened himself to murdered innocents. Despite the fire blazing in the hearth, a chill ran through him, deadly with rage.

'Come on Joe – no arsing about, just the facts.'

'I got the info from old Larry Sykes, who ses they've got police dogs sniffin' every parcel at London Road. Yer must've seen the traffic hold-ups? Anyway, Larry ses the fella wot did it, chopped 'em up and parcelled 'em off somewhere.' Joe took a drink from his pint. 'When 'e said Superintendent 'Ammond's delighted with the quick detection skills of his man – I thought you'd pleased 'im at long last.' Joe's smile faded. 'Not you after all then lad?'

'Nope. Not me.'

Joe checked his watch. 'Sit down then, and finish yer drink. I've got 'alf'an'hour before the intermission.' Joe worked as usher in the cinema next door to the pub.

Clayton shook his head. 'You have my pint Joe, I've lost the taste for it.'

WILSON CROSSED the road and approached one of the handlers locking the cage at the rear of his van. He flashed his warrant; the handler glanced then looked into Wilson's eyes.

'Off duty?'

'No,' Wilson was taken aback. No one had questioned his warrant before. 'Acting Detective Inspector, I'm under training by Superintendent Hammond. C.I.D.'

'Ah – so this is your case?'

'Yeh. How's the search going?'

'Nothing there – not in the trains or down at the Post Office. I think the search is being called off.'

'Called off – not whilst I'm in charge it isn't.' Wilson turned around, crossed to the side street where he'd left his car and headed back to Lever Street. He saw Hutton running down the steps – dressed as though heading for home. Wilson steered the car to the curb edge and braked. He wound down the window.

'What'ya doin' here Hutton, has Davies finished interviewing MacLean?'

'Yes Sir, he's bein' released.'

'What'ya talkin' about *released?*'

Hutton pointed back towards the station. 'See them blokes on the steps? Newspaper reporters – they're causin' a right stink. MacLean's Union sent their solicitor. He's got Superintendent 'Ammond by the short'n'curlies.' He lowered his voice, 'They're callin' fer you to be disciplined for strikin' their client.'

'Did you tell 'em it was me?'

'Didn't 'ave to – Davies reported you, the moment you left for the Infirmary.'

'Infir..oh yeh, not had time.' He rubbed the back of his head; the lump throbbing fit to burst.

Hutton bent towards the window and said in a low voice, 'Did you know they've called the search off.'

'Shit.' Wilson revved the engine and shot away from the curb tyres screeching and knocking Hutton sideways. Hutton stared after him – a couple of reporters ran down the steps scribbling the details of the car's number plate. One sidled up to Hutton and asked if he had anything to add to his previous comment.

BARRY BROCKLEHURST broke through the crowd of people eager to give the police details of the traffic victim and her missing children; he grabbed Clayton by the arm.

'Quick word in your ear Ian – my mate over in Minshull Street's warned the shit's about to hit the fan with Hammond.'

'Is it true B.B., are the children dead?'

'If they are – they're not in any parcel – and this lot,' he thumbed to the throng, 'say the kids've been seen alive – all in shops in different parts of Manchester mind, but seen alive.'

'It's just that, well Joe said they'd been mutilated.'

'Nah – that'll be the press – they're flocking in from everywhere – causing mischief if you ask me. But be careful of Hammond – he's likely to blow. Tell you more when I know. Bringing Wilson back's not helped the stupid sod.'

Clayton stopped dead: all around people were talking above the chaos of the night each jostling for attention – wanting someone to hear their story. He stared at B.B. felt the huge man's hand still gripping his arm.

'Wilson?'

'Yeh – before your time Ian, turned into a no good loser – hasn't changed from all accounts – still thinks with his fists.'

'Wilson from Yorkshire?'

B.B. directed an old lady towards the desk, told her to stand in the queue, 'Anyway, don't worry about Wilson, just wanted to warn you about Hammond. My mate'll let us know what he can. Got to go.'

'Can you trust your mate?'

'With me life, Ian. With me life.'

Hammond was too busy to notice Clayton's return but when Davies spotted him he put a finger to his lips and gestured shush. Clayton got the message and slid behind the filing cabinets approaching their desks from a different angle. Raised voices vibrated the glass in Hammond's office windows.

'Summat's not right,' whispered Davies. 'The Super put an outsider on our case an' e's arrested an innocent man for takin' the kids.'

Clayton looked towards the glass box. Hammond didn't look well. 'Is this outsider called Wilson?'

Davies let his breath empty from his lungs. 'Yes Sir, wasn't sure yer knew 'im. Not very nice is 'e?' he inclined his head, 'bit like the Super. 'E's in 'orrible mood – bin screamin' for'yer.'

Clayton glanced at his boss again, piecing together the information he'd received that evening. He stared at the fat neck swelling over the shirt collar. A vision of Hammond's purple head bursting and going splat against the walls brought a smile to his lips.

'Where *is* this Wilson guy?'

''E's a madman Sir, the Super made me assist him in the interview room and he lashed out at the poor fella. Don't think D.I. Wilson's thought this case through. Super's goin' to 'ave to let MacLean go.'

'MacLean?'

'Yeh, lives in the flat above the Doll's 'Ospital: Wilson's had it ripped apart. D.I. Parker ses this Wilson's goin' to cause trouble for 'Ammond an' we'll all cop for it.'

'I think Parker's dead right, but in the meantime remember Superintendent Hammond has a rank which commands respect. So no more gossip.'

'Yes Sir.'

'Having said that, what d'ya know about Wilson?'

'Nowt really, seems to 'ave come from nowhere. Parker ses he's an' old pal of the Super's.'

Over Davies's shoulder Clayton could see that the men in Hammond's office held the upper hand, and that the Super didn't like it.

'Union men,' whispered Davies. 'Brought their legal representative. He's dead good – I've been listenin' to 'im – knows 'is stuff.'

Clayton was listening and nodded whilst running a finger down the spine of files placed by Davies on his blotter. He found the one he wanted and pulled it out.

'Did you manage to re-interview the people from the offices either side of the Doll's Hospital and the tenants of Lincoln House?'

'Yes and no, those are from the offices,' he pointed to the file in front of Clayton, 'but most of the tenants had gone to work. Uniform said they'd finish off this evening.' Davies rolled his eyes, 'If there's any point.'

'What d'you mean by that?'

'Well Sir – that Wilson chap's not made us very popular 'as 'e? By all accounts, MacLean's flat's in a right mess.'

'Where's the paperwork leading to MacLean's arrest?'

'Isn't any, Mr Sharples reported noises coming from the flat and the Super sent Wilson straight out. When they broke in – couldn't find owt – dead clean said D.I. Parker.'

Hammond's voice grew louder as the office door opened, 'You have no rights!' he bawled. The suited men began to file out. Hammond's voice rising, 'The public expect to be protected from scum like him.' As the last man stepped over the threshold, Hammond slammed the door shut – shaking the metal framework. Triumphant, the men walked past Davies and Clayton's desk and left the office of the Criminal Investigation Department quietly, closing the door behind them.

'And where the hell have *you* been all evening?'

Clayton looked up; his boss's features toned with shades of purple. Before he could reply, the man leading the delegation returned and addressed Hammond.

'Mr MacLean is ready to leave the station but his keys are not amongst his personal possessions; see they are returned. There's no urgency as we believe his home has been rendered unfit for him to live in. The Union's arranged hotel accommodation until the flat's been restored. Goodnight Superintendent.' The lawyer turned to leave.

All eyes were on Hammond. 'Now just a minute,' he roared, 'MacLean stays put until the searches at the depot have been carried out. There's a lynch-mob outside this station and if we don't appear to do justice by them – they'll take the law into their own hands.'

The lawyer stood composed; in contrast to the flushed and sweating Superintendent, he said, 'And they will be showing a similar contempt for the law that you and your officers have shown this evening.' He looked around the room, 'My apologies to those not involved in this evening's disgraceful performance.' He retraced his steps and closed the door behind him.

Hammond picked up the nearest object to hand and threw it at the door where it smashed on impact. He turned to Davies, 'Get that cleaned up.' Looked around and yelled, 'You lot can piss off home for what use you are.' He grabbed his coat and stormed out.

WILSON STOOD outside the entrance to the Parcel Depot. All police presence gone now the search had been called off. The steps leading to the railway station where he and the Greek had fought were quiet and empty of people. He climbed them, made his way to the station's cafeteria and ordered coffee. Travellers dragged suitcases across platforms and grumbled about the delays and changes to timetables. He searched for somewhere to sit. A table came free when a family rose after hearing the announcement of their train; he grabbed it and sat on one of the warm seats. Another man grabbed the seat opposite. The waitress brought their drinks to the table, cleared the previous crockery and handed the newspaper left by them to Wilson.

Staring above the fold of the front page were the eyes of his wife.

Unmistakably Kathleen's – his heart leapt. Yes – it's her. Eager to read more he opened up the paper and read the caption below the sketch. *…has since died from her injuries. If anyone has information…* He shot up from his chair, the coffee spilling into the saucer and walked back to the steps leading down to the road. He'd prayed so many times for the woman to be Kathleen. Planned how he was going to beg her forgiveness – even to seek help for his rage. His prayer had been answered – the woman was Kathleen – what he omitted to ask of the gods was to say *let it be Kathleen alive.*

He'd left his car tucked down the side street at the rear of Lincoln House. He got in and lit a cigarette – blue smoke rolled across the windscreen picking up the gloom of the faint street light. Kathleen whirled inside his head – not dead on a mortuary slab – but alive and smiling. She bent toward him and kissed him full on the mouth – he could smell the perfume of her hair.

'I'm sorry,' he croaked.

Shush its okay Mike.

He shook his head his throat on fire, tears tickling the side of his nose. He let them be – his wife kissed them he felt her soft lips move over his face, just as they'd done so many times.

'Forgive me.'

I forgive you Mike.

Tears did not distort the image inside his mind, that of his beautiful wife, happy dancing and full of love just for him – just for him. She pressed her naked body next to his – he felt her lips caress the hairs on his chest. She looked up and her face had changed.

A sob – loud and mournful filled the car's interior. Unchecked the tears ran down Wilson's face and another loud sob relieved the aching in his throat – but not his chest. The unsmoked cigarette held between lifeless fingers burned deep into the fabric of his coat. The image filling his mind was battered and bruised; swollen lips and eyes. He tried to shut it out but it remained searching his face for an answer. He had none.

> 'Forgive me,' he sobbed.
> *I forgive you Mike – I forgive you.*
> 'I don't deserve you.'
> *But I love you. Always have done.*

The image kept on changing. This time no love glowed in those swollen eyes. No more would Kathleen say she forgave him. He couldn't remember the kid coming between them. Didn't know he'd swiped her away, smashing her hard against the wall. Not until Kathleen swung back, blooded and screaming with a piece of broken furniture in her hand. Screaming for him never to lay a finger on the child again – he hadn't – well not intentional: she just got in the way.

'Jesus Christ!' The cigarette burnt the thick yellow skin between his fingers. He jumped out of the car. Sparks blew away from the singed hole in his coat. Reality cleared his mind. Kathleen was dead – and someone had hold of his kids. Back in the car, he switched on the engine and drove across the city's empty streets. He needed to know more, he'd rushed things, not thought things through. Go back to the accident, he told himself, Christ – so much time wasted but Johnson would know. He and Jenkins were the first on the scene.

HAMMOND STARED at his reflection: bloated and flushed around the gills of late. A holiday was what he needed but now was not the time. He'd hoped Wilson might have lightened the load but it had been a mistake. Even Jenkins had said as much, even urged Hammond to send him back to

Yorkshire. He gave the mirror's image a tired smile. Jenkins worried about his pension – he needed to with *his* past.

He poured the whiskey into the smudged glass, topped it with a little water and looked around the room. How long had it been since his last overnight stay? Too long, but it was good to be home; he raised his glass, saluted his reflection and took a good gulp. Alfredo Boss would return any day demanding to know what he'd done about the bloody Greeks. And the paymasters at Furness Crain's office were acting strange these days. Wanting to know where the key witnesses had gone. How the fuck should he know? He took another mouthful – someone was shielding them. And bloody Gould was proving a nightmare – how cruel could fate be to have the prosecution's top silk involved in a traffic accident that gave him the perfect excuse to complain to the Chief Constable?

Now the eyes of Head Office were on his station – on his department, watching Hammond's every move. The whiskey was taking effect; he began to shut out the problems of work and allowed it to relax his mind. His own retirement had flashed in his thoughts these last weeks – he could afford it, the place in Portugal was finished and waiting for him. He swirled the amber liquid around the sides of his glass and frowned. Greasy smudges covered the crystal, he held it to the lamp, the ring he wore cut deep into his finger emphasising his recent weight gain. The moment Alfredo's case was over – he'd put his mind to dieting.

He padded through the soft carpet, discarded the dirty glass and replaced it. Shouldn't let the bastards get to him, for bastards they were every last one of them. Alfredo Boss was a habitual fraudster, by rights he deserved to go to bloody prison. How many times had Hammond engineered his acquittal?

Moving from the drinks cupboard he stopped at the mirror, circles under his eyes caught his attention. He ran a finger over the puffiness gently stroking the skin smoothing the bloating away. A lock of hair fell out of place; he teased it behind his ear, light catching the diamonds in his earrings; their sparkle bringing a smile to his lips. All his current worries fell away; Hammond loved diamonds; especially those bought for him as a show of appreciation from a generous judge – no more than he deserved – another wanker saved from prison. He shook his head to make them sparkle then turned to watch the light do the same for the necklace. Diamonds again – bought with Alfredo's money after he claimed a fortune for a shipload of scrap iron. He raised his glass saw the tips of his fingers and realised where the smudges came from – eye make-up – it's a bugger.

Perfumed air lingered in the bathroom, Hammond dried his hands picked up his glass and stopped at the full length mirror by the door; delighting in its image. He twisted round – checked the seams of his stockings were straight. They were but nevertheless he placed his glass on the ledge, lifted the hem of his crepe dress and fiddled with the suspenders. He straightened; ran both hands over his hips, feeling the silk lining cool against his naked skin. A bulge spoilt the line of the dress, 'don't think I can't see you,' he warned, 'you naughty boy.'

WILSON HAMMERED on the door again, when Florrie Jenkins eventually opened it he didn't wait to be invited in just pushed past.

'Jim's not home,' she told him.
'Is he working?'

'No,' she closed the door and followed him into the living room. Florrie knew Wilson from the old days; used to pity him but not any more. Jim had told her about the rumours coming from Leeds and the way Wilson had treated his wife. 'He's gone over to Johnny's place – something's happened at the station and they're worried they'll be disciplined.'

'Yeh they need to be. If they'd paid attention to the doll mender, MacLean might've been caught red handed.' He turned to leave and spotted a bunch of keys on the sideboard – the muddy knitted gollywog on the ring drawing his eye. 'Called at Johnny's but no one in, he is still living in Chorlton, isn't he?'

'Yeh – he'll never move far from Sally.'

Pain gripped Wilson's chest – would Kathleen be buried in the same cemetery? He shook his mind clear. Now all that remained for him was to find the children. Without another word he returned to his car and drove away. Florrie watched him go: not happy that he'd returned to Manchester with visions of the old days and the return of Jim's nightmares coming to the fore.

During the drive, Wilson had had time to think – his mind gaining clarity by the hour. Neither Jenkins nor Johnson had an inkling Kathleen had the kids with her, they'd have said so, being old mates – wouldn't they? No – it had to be something else – could the kids have been lured before Kathleen crossed the road? Lured by someone who'd befriended their mother, someone she felt was safe – some kind old man, say, with a shop full of toys.

The doll mender.

No, if he'd got the kids, he wouldn't have mentioned their existence to Johnson. Wouldn't have drawn attention to himself – it had to be MacLean. You only had to look at his eyes to know he wasn't right. But where would he take them?

And having got them there – what would he do to them? Memories of past cases tried to edge into Wilson's mind – he knocked them aside to concentrate on his missing girls. They'd vanished so quickly that no one at the scene of the accident saw them. The entrance to Lincoln House was nearest to the traffic lights – it had to be there.

THE DOOR to flat four was locked – a row raged in the flat across the landing, a woman's voice screeching and a piece of crockery smashed – married bliss thought Wilson. Pain caused him to falter on the stairs, he took a deep breath – it dug deep, worse than heartache. He'd thought he'd suffered enough in the past three years – but apparently not – can a heart actually break? And Lincoln House gave him the creeps making it hard to keep his mind focused on the job. He returned to the ground floor and looked down the hall and to Albert's flat. Always in darkness; couldn't make out whether the door was open or not. Everyone in the place was weird – like it was compulsory for the rental agreement.

He paused by the Doll's Hospital door – the last place his children had been seen. He gripped the brass handle. With a quick look around the hall he put his shoulder to the door and turned the knob. Up the stairs, another crash sounded, the fight in the flat on the first floor muffling Wilson's entry when he fell in. He closed the door and using the light from the streetlamps, crept behind the counter and entered the workshop. He lit a cigarette the flame from the Ronson catching the eyes of the teddy bears hanging from a rack above his head. Jesus – talk about the shits, Wilson inhaled, allowing the nicotine to surge through his veins, calm his nerves.

He stared around the room. Light borrowed from outside settling on ringlets of toffee coloured wood shavings scattered around a lathe, and jars of glass eyes staring in all directions from the shelf above. Stacked between two of those jars, a pile of photographs caught Wilson's eye, keeping the cigarette in his mouth he reached up for them. Dealing them one by one Wilson placed each photo of a child onto the bench, behind his ears a throb drummed with a menacing rhythm. Bingo.

How many perverts had Wilson sniffed out? Countless; but how did he miss this one? Come to think of it Oliver Sharples even *looked* the part with his benign countenance and cute glasses perched on the end of his nose. Children *would* trust him; allow him to get close. How often had he told fellow colleagues not to look for monsters when solving a child molesting case? Find the kindly uncle, trusted Priest or friendly man next door. He'd have seen it sooner if Hammond hadn't rushed him, if Sharples hadn't diverted their attention onto the poor deaf bloke. Wilson looked up at the ceiling and stared at the stain, anything, he thought, could have caused that.

Finding a large envelope, Wilson scooped the photographs into it and addressed it to Superintendent Hammond. There'd be no talk of disciplinary action now. His back will be slapped like the old times, good old Wilson hasn't lost his touch after all, they'd say.

The telephone directory gave him Sharples's home address; he dropped the envelope into Piccadilly's police box and headed out of town. The tide was turning and with luck he'd find the girls at Sharples's house. Another sharp pang seared his chest, he wondered whether investigations made into those children featured in the photographs would find some had been reported missing, or some simply logged as having been touched inappropriately?

Wilson had seen it all before.

CHAPTER SEVEN

DETECTIVE CONSTABLE Davies lifted his morning cup of tea to his lips and slurped a good mouthful – he swallowed and let out a loud sigh of contentment. 'Perfect,' he sighed and was about to repeat the action when Clayton roared at him from across the desk.

Clayton had been in a bad mood since receiving the night shift's report.

'These photographs the Super's taken to Head Office, are they supposed to be evidence against Oliver Sharples?'

Davies had another mouthful of tea – it trickled down his throat, the feeling pleasurable and warming. Clayton waited for an answer and sat glaring at him. Davies rushed a swallow, sending some into his windpipe. Milky sweet tea sprayed across the desk as he choked. Clayton could stand no more. He shot from the office and sought the refuge of the station's canteen.

Hot toast and grilled bacon wafted up as Clayton reached the steps bumping into B.B. on the way.

'Get a cuppa for me Ian – I'll be back in a tick.'

Clayton jumped the queue, ordered two teas and a couple of Kit-Kats. Brocklehurst had found two seats by the time he fought his way across the crowded canteen.

'Got the cells full of brainless twits caught brawlin' over by the canal last night.' B.B. broke the Kit-Kat in two. 'Thank God the deaf and dumb fella's been released – these louts would 'ave killed 'im. Call 'emselves Teddy boys – bloody thugs - spots an' greasy 'air – nothing more.' He blew cold air onto the top of his tea and took a sip. 'Minshull Street's pulled 'Ammond in,' he whispered.

'I thought he'd gone over voluntarily – taken new evidence.'

'Yer mean them photos? 'Ammond's a bloody idiot. The owner of the Doll's 'Ospital makes props for the ballet. If 'Ammond 'ad looked on the back he'd have seen the kids' measurements. My mate says the whole thing would be a huge laugh only for the fact that Oliver Sharples is in Stockport Infirmary, witnesses 'ave put Mike Wilson as the man who beat him up.'

'How come Wilson's at large? Why the hell wasn't he picked up yesterday when he attacked MacLean?'

'Beats me – anyway you should be glad 'Ammond's getting his come-uppence. E'll not be able to shield Wilson this time.' B.B. took another sip, 'You coming on the trip Thursday night?'

'Yeh, I'd forgotten,' Clayton opened his wallet and gave B.B. a note. 'Get me a ticket.'

'Not got anything smaller?'

'The change'll cover my bets – back to Wilson – what d'you mean - shield him this time?'

B.B. pocketed the money and picked up the other half of the Kit-Kat. 'Official story is – a suspect resisting arrest fell and broke his neck. Others say Wilson lost it and lay into the suspect. Jenkins spoke up for Wilson but we all knew it was iffy.'

''Cos Jenkins and Wilson never got on?'

'Understatement, anyway, after that, 'Ammond moved mountains to shift Wilson sideways and cover the tracks.'

'Then why bring him back?' Clayton didn't bother to lower his voice, the clatter of the canteen made it almost impossible to hear B.B.'s words. 'From what I hear - Hammond keeps bad company as it is – he doesn't need Wilson.'

Brocklehurst nodded, ''Ammond attracts bad company. He's a nasty little shit if you want my opinion. But like he protects Wilson, someone higher, watches over him.'

'Until now.'

B.B. nodded, 'Finger's crossed.'

On Clayton's return he stopped by to speak to Doreen, the C.I.D. typist. 'Just the girl I need,' he told her, 'tell me what you know about this Wilson fella.'

'Well, he's single, on transfer from Yorkshire, arrived last Thursday, taken Hardcastle's job and is training to be a Detective Inspector.'

'Hardcastle?'

'Don't give me that Ian Clayton – you know Hardcastle.' She rolled her eyes when he shook his head. 'You can't've forgotten the New Year before last – you fished him out of the Irwell.'

He burst into laughter at the memory. 'And we both received a load of injections because the water's so filthy. You're right – I do remember just forgot the name. Why's he on leave?'

'His wife's sister's really poorly – she's gone to Leeds to care for her. Hardcastle put in for transfer and the Super fixed it.'

'If Wilson's under training, whose he placed with?'

'Supposed to be the Super, I think. They spend a lot of time together.'

'What does he look like?'

Doreen smiled, 'I like him. He's not as tall as you but quite muscular – sort of rugged.'

'He's a nasty piece of work. Keep out of his way.'

'Oh you're just as bad as the others. He just needs a little love and friendship.'

Clayton put his arm around Doreen's shoulders. 'We all need a little love and friendship Doreen, but you'll not find it in Wilson – he's bad news; trust me.'

Davies had papers spread out to dry on top of the filing cabinet and the desk spotless when Clayton returned.

'Summat's not right 'ere.' He grumbled to Clayton, 'Things keep goin' missin'.'

'Like what?'

'The Pathology report concerning the traffic victim, I put it here for you to read and it's gone.'

'What did it say?'

'Injuries received by the car might not 'ave caused 'er death. Further tests were to be carried out.' Davies looked up from the stack of papers. 'She'd suffered quite a few broken bones in the past – not all of 'em set properly.' Clayton nodded but said nothing.

'Sir – are we still on the case?'

Clayton smiled, looked at the vacant office where Hammond should be. 'Yes, until someone takes us off it. I want to interview MacLean. Get me what you know about him.'

The phone rang; Davies picked it up and handed it to Clayton. B.B.'s loud voice could be heard across the desk. Davies heard him tell Clayton that a call's been put out to bring Wilson in. He's to be charged with grievous bodily harm and Hammond's been suspended pending further enquiries.

CLAYTON PULLED his collar around his ears and walked towards the barrier across the entrance to the Parcel Depot.

'Oi, where d'you think you're goin'?' yelled the guard.

Raising his warrant badge to the gatehouse window he replied, 'D.I. Clayton, I wish to see Mr MacLean.'

The man hissed through his teeth. 'Why can't you leave 'im alone?   Nowt but sheer prejudice what you're doin'. Stay 'ere – I'll fetch the supervisor.' The gateman spoke into the phone. 'Mr Dean, I've got a copper at the gate, ses he wants to see David.' He paused, replaced the receiver and pointed to where the road disappeared under the viaduct. 'Through the tunnel – you'll find the depot on the right.'

The attitude of Dean, MacLean's supervisor was hostile, but Clayton's mood was no better.

'David's spent hours in your stinkin' cells,' Dean bleated on, 'his flat's a wreck and he's got a thick lip.'

Clayton took a deep breath. 'I just want to ask some questions. It'll take a couple of minutes – if Mr MacLean prefers, he can always come to the station.'

Dean scoffed, led Clayton past trolleys stacked with mountains of parcels waiting to be sorted. Ahead, a man lifted a package onto the platform of a three-wheeled truck. He had his back to them Dean tapped him on the shoulder, scribbled a note and waved Clayton on when the man gave a nod.

'Use this,' the supervisor handed a notepad and pencil, ''e's deaf – not stupid, he'll answer your questions as well as any man.'

MacLean sat on the edge of the trolley, pulled his own notepad from his overall pocket and waited.

WERE YOU AT THE TRAFFIC LIGHTS ON MONDAY EVENING? MacLean shook his head. Clayton was drawn to MacLean's stark eyes and the comments made by Davies about Wilson not liking them. A MAN MATCHING YOUR DESCRIPTION WAS PUSHING HIS WAY TOWARDS THE LADY BEFORE SHE WAS KNOCKED DOWN. WAS IT YOU? Maintaining his haunting stare MacLean shook his head. WHERE WERE YOU? He pointed to his workbench.

DID YOU LEAVE THE DEPOT? Slowly, MacLean shook his head. Clayton's enquiries revealed the depot worker had not taken the Union's offer of hotel accommodation. He wiped his fingers across his mouth and wrote. WHERE DID YOU SLEEP LAST NIGHT?

Taking the pencil in his left hand MacLean scrawled, Flat 4 Lincoln House

I THOUGHT IT WAS A MESS? Clayton detected a hint of annoyance as the man scribbled his answer.

Not even the efforts of Sergeant Wilson can drive me from my home.

Ouch, thought Clayton, *did I touch a nerve?* He looked into MacLean's eyes and saw he struggled to regain his composure. Why did he refer to Wilson as Sergeant when he's known as a D.I.? He wrote, I WISH TO SEE THE FLAT.

Is this to do with the blind man?

WHY DO YOU ASK? MacLean shrugged his shoulders; realised Clayton waited for an answer and wrote.

He doesn't like me. I can't hear his swearing.

Davies had told Clayton about Albert's colourful language, he smiled.

DON'T KNOW HOW LUCKY YOU ARE The strange blue eyes softened and a smile spread across the depot worker's lips until the split given by Wilson's signet ring made him scowl.

I finish work at 5.30.

CHAPTER EIGHT

HIGH ABOVE the gaming tables Bernardo Boss oversaw the final preparations to his new nightclub –and smiled. His office: nicknamed the *eagle's nest* offered the perfect view from where he could observe who came and went and how much money was won or lost. Chandeliers: a special import from Palermo via Bernardo's Sicilian friends hung above each roulette table – their opaque translucent lustre reflected on each table's edge. And the pearl theme continued; picked up by the mirrors behind the Oyster Bar and washed across its mother of pearl surfaces.

Bernardo's attention was taken away from the casino by a movement near the entrance where two men were trying to get past his business partner, Andy Burke. When Bernardo recognised Superintendent Hammond accompanied by some tow-rag of a plain clothed copper, he winced, took a deep breath and headed down the spiral staircase to meet them.

'It's okay Andy, I'll see the Superintendent and his friend in the Oyster Bar.' Bernardo pointed the way and Burke stood aside for the unwelcome guests. The policemen shuffled past – Hammond sweaty and nervous – Wilson edgy and dishevelled. Their appearance contrasting sharply with Bernardo and Burke's groomed style and relatively relaxed composure. 'You are welcome of course,' Bernardo told them, 'but please make your visit brief, I have much to do before the grand opening.'

Hammond coughed. 'Gould's stirring mischief with Henderson leaving my station under the siege of the press. We'll have to cool things until it blows over.'

'We don't have the luxury of waiting for anything to blow over. The trial's due to be heard in the spring and cannot take another postponement. My brother expects you to cover things from your end and, as we know, rewards you in advance for your endeavours.' Bernardo walked behind the bar and poured a whiskey. 'Would you gentlemen care to join me?'

'A large scotch small jug of water,' said Hammond, 'my colleague doesn't drink, though he does have other vices.'

Wilson pulled Hammond's sleeve. 'We've important things to do, it would be better if you didn't stink of whiskey.'

Hammond snatched his sleeve free and turned his attention to Bernardo. 'As soon as the limelight's off my department – I'll track the Greeks down and silence 'em.'

'Like you did with the boatyard family?' Bernardo handed a glass with a generous measure of whiskey towards Hammond; followed by the water.

'It worked didn't it – got your brother off?' Hammond knocked back a good slug, the burn to his throat easing the grilling he'd received at Head Office.

'Superintendent Hammond; you seem to forget how my brother once earned his living. He doesn't pay you for your physical prowess, he pays you to break the rules, filter the evidence and find those in hiding. My brother's lawyers need time to prepare his defence – your job is destroying evidence against him. Now, if you will excuse me – I've work to do.'

'I wanted Alfredo to know how the situation lies at Lever Street, that's all. Also, my colleague here has got into a spot of trouble.' Hammond placed a photograph of Wilson on the bar, 'he may need to leave the country unnoticed.' He knocked back the remaining scotch.

Bernardo looked across to where Wilson had wandered. 'What's he done?'

'Don't get me wrong, he's a good lad to have around – but a bit quick with the old fists, if you get my drift.'

'He's killed someone.'

'Not this time, but very nearly and I want him out of my hair.' Hammond caught Bernardo's stifled laugh and felt his coal black eyes on his scalp. 'Yeh well, I was using a figure of speech.'

'I'll see what I can do,' Bernardo picked up the photo and tucked it into his top pocket. 'The cost to be borne by you, tell him to call into the Grey Flamingo tomorrow evening. Now back to the subject in hand; why can't you dig up some dirt on Gould? After all, isn't that where you excel? Finding grubby bits and pieces about people and using it to make them reconsider was always your forte.' Bernardo took a sip of whiskey. 'Maybe you've lost your touch Superintendent.' The look he gave the policeman left him in no doubt how intense his dislike was. Bernardo despised what Hammond did on behalf of the law firm his brother used and hoped this to be the last time Alfredo had need of their services.

Wilson returned to the bar, Bernardo stared into his eyes, and was reminded of the vacant look ex boxers got when they'd taken too many punches. Hammond had left the bar and waited by the entrance – Wilson followed, paused to say something to Burke then changed his mind. Without physical contact, Burke spread his arms wide and directed the man back on course and onto the street.

Bernardo smiled – Burke was the best in the business and priceless. He returned to the eyrie and made arrangements to furnish Wilson with a false passport. After which, he did his best to rid his mind of Superintendent Hammond and his pathetic looking assistant. The next distraction by the entrance to *Pearl's Nightclub* came when Burke and Alfredo embraced like brothers. Bernardo ran down to greet him – threw the keys to Burke and took his brother on a tour of the night club then to lunch at Mario's Ristorante where they could eat, drink and talk in private.

SUPERINTENDENT BENSON concluded the disciplinary lecture and ordered Sergeants Johnson and Jenkins out of his office. Colleagues gave the pair no eye contact as they made their way to the station's car park and loaded the van with road cones. Menial traffic duties for the foreseeable future Benson had told them – all because they didn't believe the woman had a couple of kids with her.

'This is Wilson's fault,' said Jenkins, 'what business had he to beat old Sharples?'

Johnson slammed the back doors, pulled a twenty pack of Senior Service from his pocket and sat in the driver's seat. Jenkins was too ready to blame Wilson – always had been.

'Told you he'd blow it,' Jenkins's continued, throwing his raincoat behind the passenger seat and climbing in, 'knuckles instead of brains – that's bloody Wilson.'

Johnson reversed out of the slot, gave a curt nod to the reporters gathered in the car park and drove on. 'Mike must've gone straight to Sharples's 'ouse after callin' at your place.'

'Yeh, Florrie said he was looking for trouble – said his face was sore – like he'd been fighting and eyes red – full of anger. Didn't say what he wanted – just barged in and stormed out. You can't tell where he'll go next – he's like a bloody pin-ball.'

Johnson pulled in by the curb. 'I need fags, won't be long.' He returned with a newspaper – headlines giving details of Oliver Sharples's attacker and a photograph of Wilson as a Sergeant in uniform. Johnson took the last two cigarettes from the old pack and handed one to Jenkins.

'The paper-shop's full – Mike's big news at the moment and 'Ammond's bin suspended.' His lighter lit the murky cab's interior – outside, storm clouds brought the evening dark earlier than scheduled. ''Enderson's got men combing the files at Lever Street. They're delvin' into Wilson's past.'

'Shit – what about my pension?'

'Sod your fuckin' pension Jim, if 'Ammond squeals – we'll be spending our retirement behind bars: or worse.'

Jenkins inhaled: his eyes on the photograph of Wilson, taken a few years back and presumably given to the journalist by Yorkshire police. 'That was a long time ago Johnny, Henderson's not interested in delving that far back.'

'Yeh, well remember this, killin' a police officer's an'angin' offence.'

'Hammond made me hit him – anyway Mike didn't die.'

Johnson brought the van's engine into life and continued to the road works, where they'd been ordered to keep the evening traffic flowing too and from Manchester's Ship Canal.

113

CLAYTON WROTE down the information given by Somerset House and fed more coins into the slot. He pressed the clerk with more questions and was told to hold – outside a queue waited to use the phone. If Whiteman's tip about Kathleen having relatives in Manchester was correct – then there was hope the children could be with them. Kathleen's maiden name was Williams – his money ran out. Bloody Williams – there were thousands of folk called Williams. He pushed the sprung kiosk door open and held it for the man waiting patiently in the cold.

DAVIES SIFTED through the sheets of statements given by the residents housed in the terraced buildings on London Road. Clayton handed him a cake and went to put on the kettle.

'Sir?'

'Mmm.'

'These workers from the solicitor's office in Lincoln 'Ouse?'

'Yeh, what about them?' Clayton wondered whether he and Davies had started to share thoughts.

'I've interviewed 'em twice an' each time they said they finished work at five and closed the office at five fifteen, yet….'

'Last Monday they were delayed by a client.'

'Yessir, 'ow did you know what I was gonna say?'

'Work with em long enough, Davies – great minds and all that.' Clayton brewed the tea and gave it a stir. He checked his watch. 'I'm takin' a stroll over to Lincoln House this evening, want another word with MacLean – I'll pop in the solicitors, get what I can on that client.' He poured the tea and carried the chipped and cracked mugs to their desk. 'Where's my cup?'

'Super smashed it against the door, remember?'
'Aye.'

THE UNIFORMED officer looked flustered as he approached Doreen's desk. She looked up from her typewriter.

'Can I help you, Constable Hutton?'

'Yeh, which desk is O'Brien's?'

She pointed it out, 'It's the one in the corner, he's around somewhere.'

'I know but he's busy. I've been asked to collect some things from the drawer.' He pulled open the bottom one. 'Got a large envelope?'

'Those things belong to D.I. Wilson. They're not O'Brien's.'

'I know, its Wilson who asked for them. He's waiting in the car park.'

Doreen gave Hutton an envelope, walked to the window and looked down. She could see the van from Head Office and policemen loading boxes of files, but no sign of Wilson's car.

Hutton's hands were trembling as he folded the flap and sealed the envelope. She knew he was risking his career by helping Wilson and wondered why.

'I'll take it to him if you like,' she volunteered, 'could do with a breath of fresh air.'

'You sure?' he asked, 'he's not in a good mood.'

'What's the matter with you men, can't anyone think of anything nice to say about him?' She snatched the envelope from Hutton, turned away and left the office.

CHAPTER NINE

BERNARDO PLACED a hand over his glass preventing Mario from topping it up. He sat back and watched him re-fill Alfredo's who was on form – bursting with news of his trip. Mario swapped Italian jokes with Alfredo – old and no longer funny. Bernardo stifled a yawn – lunch with Alfredo ran to the same pattern. Measuring time by volume of wine consumed – he reckoned his brother's clock was running fast. Soon the melodrama of the war years would begin and Mario and Alfredo would shed tears over their families' losses. With pride Alfredo would re-count how their family had aided the partisans' raids during the occupation of their village. And through bitter tears would tell of loved ones brought down by the firing squads.

Bernardo glanced through the window, stared onto the cold pavement and the passers-by wrapped up in their winter clothes. As far as he was concerned, those days were over and now, Manchester was his home – he'd attended its famous grammar school and built a good life. He turned away from the window when Mario changed the subject from the war back to boxing and Alfredo's former prowess in the ring. The tears were swept away the glasses refilled and so it continued. Alfredo lived in the past – dwelt in halls of glory and dungeons of hatred – both places seething with blind prejudice.

When Mario left to attend to his busy restaurant and Alfredo appeared to have sated his lust for things past, Bernardo coughed and brought the conversation to the present.

'Furness, Crane and Neilson aren't going to get you off this time Alfredo. Superintendent Hammond is struggling to keep pace. I think he's washed out.'

'He's been paid – so he'll deliver.'

'No he won't – not this time. Andy and I have cleaned what we can from your side of the business, but you've got to be prepared to let the…er…shall we say, shady aspects go.'

'Shady aspects?' Alfredo's look was mean – the wine souring his nature. 'You were never so fussy when I paid for your fancy education. Did I ever hear reference to shady aspects when you and Burke were on the ski slopes – acting like playboys at my expense? No.'

'But times have changed, anyway it was you insisted I be brought up to be a gentleman – I didn't ask for it.' Bernardo gave his watch a side-glance. Another glass of wine and Pauline would be brought into the conversation – Alfredo hated Bernardo's wife.

'You didn't ask for it no,' Alfredo shook his head and stared into his glass, 'but it was intended to give you what I never had: and for my part, a complete waste of money.' He placed the rim to his lips and slammed down the glass without drinking. 'Did it teach you to woo a Countess? No. You married that stuck up bitch that stinks of horse-shit.'

The insults came early – Bernardo surmised Alfredo must have had a few brandies on the Pullman from London. He stood up to leave; nothing to be gained business-wise, once Alfredo got his teeth into Pauline.

Mario returned from the kitchen, two brandy glasses in one hand and a bottle from his top shelf in the other. He gave Bernardo the wink, which always meant, you go now – and leave your stupid old brother to me.

MR DEAN scowled when Clayton entered the subterranean sorting office of the Parcel Depot; and threatened to bring the Union's legal might if Lever Street continued harassing his employee.

'I'm not harassing David, honest – it's just that we'd agreed to meet later and I've been given another case,' lied Clayton.

Mr Dean shrugged his shoulders, 'Well Inspector, you're too late, David's shift ended an hour ago.'

'I thought it ended at 5.30?'

'It does when he's working the middle shift,' said Dean as he lifted a parcel onto the waiting cart, 'but he's on earlies for the next six days.'

Clayton nodded showing none of the irritation running inside his head. MacLean had lied to him again. 'Pity,' he said, 'I'll have to catch him another time.' He turned to leave, 'You know Mr Dean, I'm not happy about the treatment Mr MacLean received at my station, and I know it's a feeble excuse, but when a couple of little girls go missing..,' he detected a slight pause in Dean's movements, 'things get a little fraught.'

'Yeh – well David's been cleared. You should leave him alone.'

'I'd like to, but there's something in his statement which we need to clarify. It isn't easy when everything has to be written down.'

'We manage well enough – being deaf and dumb doesn't make him a child molester. In fact David's babysat for most of the lads in the depot. Their kids think the world of him.'

Dean's support for an employee was commendable, a virtue in Clayton's opinion, he changed tactic. 'Do you have children Mr Dean?'

'Yeh but mine are beyond the need for a sitter.'

Clayton smiled, 'I wasn't thinking of Mr MacLean, I just wanted to ask how you'd feel if it was your three year old and eight year old gone missing for days.'

'I'd be devastated – but wouldn't expect you to lash out at innocent people.'

'The officer responsible will be disciplined,' Clayton hoped. 'In the meantime, I must press on. My job is asking questions but like I said it isn't easy with someone who's deaf and dumb.'

'If you'd shown David a little patience in the first place, instead of...' Dean wiped his hands down the sides of his overall, '...hitting him, he'd have answered anything you wanted. He's the kindest soul in the world, for goodness sake; he nursed his aunt better than anyone could. Ask any of the lads, they'll tell you how good he is with their kids. Mine are grown up but still ask after him.'

'I didn't know any of this.'

'No, and you won't with the treatment he received at your station.'

'I'm sorry truly about that, did his aunt recover?'

'No, she died twelve months back, and since then the poor lad's had to put up with greedy relatives contesting the will – and now this.' Dean looked over to his men, some pausing from their work to look back.

'I see, that'll be why he visited the solicitors on Monday evening, when you said he was here.' Clayton watched the colour drain from the supervisor's face, as his words sunk in. 'You gave him an alibi which was false Mr Dean.'

'He finished early so he could sign the papers, Inspector.' Dean said lowering his voice. 'I arranged the appointment.'

Clayton leaned on one of the parcel stacks, bent his head to hear more. Dean turned his head, gave his men a quick look, Clayton followed his gaze. Dean got up nodded for Clayton to follow and the two men entered an office similar in size and structure to that of Hammond's glass box.

'Harry over there wanted to take his kids to see the switching on of the Christmas lights. He asked if he could leave early – I refused.' As though Clayton needed to know the reason he said, 'Christmas is our busiest time Inspector – everyone knows the rules – no time off.' Clayton glanced up; a couple of men looked his way – then returned to work when he stared back. 'If they found out I'd let David off early – there'd be resentment. They accuse me of overprotecting him as it is.'

'Supplying a false alibi is more than over protection, Mr Dean – it carries a jail sentence.'

Dean gulped. 'On Monday morning, David brought a letter. It was from the solicitors acting for the probate. You know it really annoys me. David and his aunt have been their clients for years – they know he can't speak – yet they wrote asking him to telephone for an appointment. I phoned on his behalf, gave them a piece of my mind.'

'This was the outcome of his aunt's will?'

'Yes, anyway February was the earliest they could see him. I yelled at them demanded to slot him in sooner. They said they could squeeze him last thing that day.' Dean rubbed his eyelids, 'I took it - David worked through his break and left early. None of this makes him a child abductor Inspector.'

'No and I don't think he is, but if I can get him to tell me the truth about that evening, he could lead me to whoever took the children.' In the sea of detection Clayton's mind held the threads of a trawler's net. He spread the net across the water.

'Tell me Mr Dean, these relatives who want to share in his aunt's will; do any of them live in Yorkshire?'

'No, *they're* okay. It's the greedy sods who live in Stretford who're after the money.' The supervisor shook his head relieved the Inspector had changed the subject from jail. 'No, David's re-union with his Yorkshire relations turned out very well, despite my warning.'

Clayton gave the mental net a little tug. 'Warning, why?'

'Aunty Ethel had brought David up as her own, single handed, which isn't easy for a spinster. His mother rejected him at birth.' Dean caught Clayton's frown, 'Oh yes Inspector, when the doctors warned of his handicap, she wanted him placed him in an institution. Ethel prevented it – refused to believe he was mentally disabled and reared the lad herself. His mother took the money Ethel gave her, enough to start a new life and never looked back.'

'I take it the new life was in Yorkshire?'

'Yes, and Ethel's other sister, who'd kept in touch, arranged the gathering a few months back. David's real mother is a widow with a couple of grown up children. I thought he'd get hurt, y'know seeing her after all those years – but he really enjoyed it.'

'Well I hope it works out for him,' Clayton let out a relaxed laugh though his mental fishing line still remained taut – and twitching. 'Y'know with the extra money, he might be able to buy a couple of rugs for that flat of his.' He held his breath.

Sensing the interview was at an end, Mr Dean relaxed, echoing Clayton's laugh. 'Oh,' he chuckled, 'now the vulture's are off David's back, he'll probably move back to Keith Street.'

'Aye, probably. Good afternoon Mr Dean.' Clayton pulled in the net, tied the loose ends and filed them ready for another time. He smiled as he left the depot.

CHAPTER TEN

IN THE inner sanctum of his heart, Hammond knew this day would come. His lucky domino had finally collapsed sending a chain reaction in every direction. The mole at the office of Furness, Crane and Neilson had given him the wink, hinted that senior partners were fluttering in panic and booking one-way tickets to far off destinations.

Now: all he felt was freedom, a kind of euphoria had entered his being and brought with it, joy. He had been released, tossed aside by everyone and left to wallow.

Opening the garage doors wide, he ran a hand over the sleek lines of the two-tone Riley and placed the basket of clean laundry on the matching cream and black leather seat. The passenger door gave a gentle click as he pushed it closed. He looked around, teased back the curls under his headscarf and gave the knot an extra tug. Naked under the calf length fur coat, its satin lining smooth against his skin, Hammond reversed the car onto the quiet lane, locked the garage doors and headed for his Cheshire 'love nest'.

WILLIAM GOULD found Faulkner sat in their usual corner of the Waldorf, deep in the newspaper by the fire.

'Did you hear what happened to poor Oliver?' he asked.

Charlie put his paper aside. 'It's my job to know things, William, I also know you've made another strong complaint to the Chief Constable.'

'I'm not going to allow them to sweep this under the carpet. The medical personnel at the Infirmary fear Oliver might lose a kidney. Where did Wilson dig up the so-called evidence? It's outrageous to suggest Oliver has a perverted liking for children. Isn't it?' Gould took off his coat and sat down. 'Ah, thanks Kenny,' he gave the whiskey a shot of soda and took a sip.

Faulkner waited whilst the waiter replaced his glass before answering. 'Trumped up,' he leaned forward giving Gould a steely glare, 'Oliver works with the theatre and especially the ballet troupe. I called to see them today, the stage manager showed me the 'jack-in-a-box' Oliver designed and made for a performance of Nutcracker. Lovely workmanship, the man's a perfectionist.'

Gould's normally impassive features relaxed. 'Oh I see, and the photographs are of children from the ballet? They're dancers.'

There were times when Faulkner despaired with Gould. For one so learned he could be slow on the uptake. 'Yes, Oliver makes the props, and he has to allow for the children's growth and the growing habits of their understudies. It was the troupe's leader took the pictures not Oliver – she also wrote the measurements for Oliver to work with.'

Gould took another sip – the relief he felt given off by a sigh. 'And what other little gems have you unearthed today?'

'You mean apart from your taxi driver getting his name in print?'

'Ted? What's he been saying?'

'Oh just that he knew all along that the victim was a mother, even though he didn't notice her children. The article reads, "My concern was for the poor lady's welfare, but the knitted toy attached to her keys had MUM embroidered across his back – so they should have taken Mr Sharples more seriously." Then it goes on to say how incompetent the police handling the case have been, blah…blah.'

Gould nodded. 'An absolute shambles, I couldn't agree more, no more snippets?'

'You know old Neilson's jumped ship – he moved out this morning. That leaves Furness and Crane to face the music. Hammond's gone – disappeared from my source's radar. Don't know how he does it – Fred, my source, says he had him one minute gone the next. Hammond's somewhere near the glove factory on the Tipfield Industrial Estate but Fred's buggered if he knows where.' Charlie tilted the glass to his mouth and stopped, remembering something else he had to say. 'Something's giving my moustache a twitch about the deaf and dumb bloke who works in the Parcel Depot.'

'Oh why, I understood he'd been released without charge?'

'Released because he had an alibi, but my investigations put him at the scene when the accident took place.'

'He lied?'

'Not only that, got his work mates to cover for him. Anyway, I'm going to my usual place later and watch his movements. Clever bugger gave me the slip last night, but he'll not do it twice.'

'So – with Hammond on the run, where does that leave our friend Alfredo Boss?'

'He's home – spent the afternoon with his Italian associates. Not much to report. Alfredo's a creature of habit – doesn't change.'

'He'll have to when he goes to prison.'

Faulkner nodded, raised his glass in triumph; his client's hard work was about to show reward at long last, he took a sip, retrieving his evening newspaper, he passed it towards Gould.

'Interesting article here, according to this journalist, the missing children could be Wilson's.'

Gould's clear blue eyes widened, he took the paper and read the article indicated by Faulkner. Pictured beside Wilson was Kathleen, his young wife. The article related to a medal awarded to Wilson for bravery. It linked Kathleen with the road victim and her missing children to Wilson.

'If Wilson reads this, finds out it's *his children* who have been abducted,' Charlie sat back, 'there's no knowing what he might do.'

JOSHUA OPENSHAW stared at the front page of his evening newspaper. The man who'd ruined his life, ruined his family's life was being hunted by his own kind. Four years in prison for a crime Joshua had not done – spent amongst rapists, perverts and arse bandits. He'd become witness to their actions – heard the statements of returned prisoners, child molesters unashamed, their only regret: they'd been caught. For four years he'd listened to their unguarded comments and grown convinced that child abusers were abused as children and once infected, their disease had no cure.

Josh read on, the journalist quoted comments made 'off the record' by ex colleagues of Wilson. How his mood swings had alienated Wilson from his mates and caused the break up of his marriage. Openshaw knew this; he knew everything there was to know about Sergeant Michael Wilson.

His years of incarceration had been put to good use. Openshaw asked for and got permission to study. His subject matter: the psychology of sexual offenders – from birth to the grave. He submitted papers but wasn't taken seriously – his views too controversial for liberal minded university professors. But Josh didn't mind this – he pressed on with his research, was given a room for study and permission to question follow inmates. Eventually, under the guise of researching the capture and treatment of offenders, he was able to obtain information about Wilson.

The policeman made a good subject for study. His past wasn't easy to unravel – but Openshaw got there in the end. He spoke to sex offenders who knew Wilson and to the guards, some sang praise for the policeman, others offered caution. But Joshua had no need to be cautious, what was there left for him to lose? And Wilson had broken the rules. With planted evidence, he and his mates had changed the way of life for all the Openshaw family forever.

He stared at the newspaper article – there was so much the world did not know about Sergeant Michael Wilson. Upon release, Josh visited Wilson's birthplace, spoke to neighbours who remembered the grandparents who raised the lad. And traced some of the children who lived at the orphanage Wilson was sent to when both grandparents died two days before his ninth birthday. Joshua Openshaw knew more about Michael Wilson than most people and he intended to use this knowledge to trap the manic policeman.

The Land Rover he was driving came to the top of the dirt track. He beeped twice on the horn and when he passed the farmhouse, turned the vehicle round. Jacob, his brother lumbered towards the Rover's back door and opened it. He placed the wicker basket by Josh's toolbox wedging it firm with their overnight bags. He gave Josh a grin, his ruddy cheeks glowing against the grey stone of the buildings, ran back to the house and brought a fleece to cover the basket.

'Look Jake, they'll be fine,' shouted their mother from the farmhouse doorway, 'God give 'em feathers ter keep 'em warm, so stop fussin'.' She gave Josh a smile and raised her eyes to heaven. 'Yer sure yer want to tek 'im? E's a blinkin' pest.'

'He's alright Ma – dunna fret.' Josh got out and gave his mother's fragile form a gentle hug. 'I'll look after 'im.'

'A know yer will lad, a'know. Tek care, both o'yer.' She lifted the hem of her apron and wiped her face mopping the tears with it. 'Come back safe'n'sound now. Safe'n'sound.'

'Just do your part Ma, okay? Get coppers 'ere in an hour,' he checked his watch, 'no, mek that half'an'hour, they've predicted snow.'

She watched Joshua drive out of the lane and closed the door. She returned to her chair and waited, the only sounds – the fire's crackle and the tick from the clock dominating the mantle shelf. Propped against it was the letter received by mail that morning – the one she intended to show to the police. Half'n'hour Josh had said, she tapped her fingers on the crisp-ironed cloth and watched the second hand click in time.

The Land Rover criss-crossed the sheep tracks, its tyres spraying icy water from hillside streams and rivulets. Flurries of snow drifted from the metal grey sky and melted on the flat glass of the vehicle's screen. Josh drove with skill and traversed the Yorkshire Moors until he reached the road linking the isolated farmhouse to the rest of the world.

DAVIES PEERED around the door and gave Doreen a frown.

'B.B. ses Wilson's been seen in the yard.'

Colour flushed her cheeks. 'He just wanted the things from his desk.'

'What things?'

She pushed back the typewriter, grabbed her handbag and stood up. '*His things,* Kevin, diaries, bits and pieces he kept in Tom's drawer.'

Davies looked towards O'Brien's desk. 'Where's Tom?'

'Dunno.' She flicked her head to one side. 'Ask Hutton, he's the one who knows everything – now move out of the way Kevin, I need the loo.'

He stepped aside. 'Tell yer what,' he called after her, ''e's got a bloody nerve.'

'Who?' O'Brien appeared from the corridor, 'and what's up with Doreen?'

Davies gave O'Brien a twisted smile. 'That Wilson, he's got a bloody nerve takin' stuff from your drawer.'

O'Brien strolled to his desk, opened the drawer used by Wilson and closed it. 'Good riddance! But he's not taken everything with him,' he bent down, picked up the standard issue green metal waste bin and tilted it for Davies to see. 'Man's a bloody nutcase, Kevin, a bloody nutcase.'

A large pink doll had been rammed into the bin, it was covered in cigarette ends, screwed up Senior Service cigarette packet and ash – the face and belly concave – crushed under the tread of a size eleven boot.

LIFTING THE record with care, Hammond placed it on the turntable and clicked the play switch. When he flexed his fingers, the polished nails picked out the pink of the soft lighting. The stylus hissed through the speaker, the music began, loud and ritzy as Marylyn Monroe's voice cooed in his ears, Hammond eyed his reflection and hummed in tune.

The image had blonde hair and a beauty spot by her lip. He thrust his chin out, cupped the curls from the back of his neck and pouted – she pouted back and giggled. *But diamonds are a girl's best friend.* He turned up the volume, took a sip from his glass and frowned at the taste of the lipstick. Loved its lustre hated the taste: he sashayed to the bathroom, red patent heels digging into the deep carpet. With care he wiped his glass clean. On his return, he stopped by a favourite spot, the full-length mirror and gave the dress another twirl. Folds of crepe georgette swayed from the hip, and swirled around noting the seams of his black silk stockings. He stopped moving and the hem, weighty and chic fell still by his shapely calves. Hammond loved the cut of this dress, loved all of his dresses.

He mooched into the bedroom: eyes catching the reflection of his large bed in the mirror hanging by chains from the ceiling. He recalled the raised eyebrow given by the interior designer when he'd asked for the mirror to be included in the alterations: and smiled. He slid the wardrobe door to one side, ran fingers over the silk underwear until they sensed the scarves. Just the feel brought a thrill. *...quite Continental...but diamonds are a.. mm...mm...mm.* Tossing the lengths of gossamer material across the bed he slid closed the wardrobe door and smiled at the returned image... *won't pay the rental on your humble flat.* The zip glided along its track, Hammond hunched both shoulders and the dress fell noiselessly to the floor, he kicked it aside, his eyes riveted on the lace suspender belt and matching panties. Free from the confines of the dress, his penis poked through the gap between pantie top and belt. *...and we all lose our charms in the end.*

Hammond pulled the silk scarf through his manicured fingers and smiled wickedly at the image before him.

'You really are a naughty boy,' he scolded giving the erect penis a slap, 'so impatient.' He gave another slap, and another dragging the scarf's length across the sensitive skin. Hammond groaned, closed his eyes for a moment and repeated the punishment. Satin – cool and sexy – soothed the friction-sore skin for one blissful moment; before the lengthy scarf tossed his penis from the suspender belt's sanctuary and rolled it back and forth – side to side gripping and stretching. Until – unable to take any more, exploded over the bejewelled hand.

'Now see what you've done! We'll have to start all over again.'

CLAYTON FOUND Keith Street with the aid of his trusty street map plus the light from the nearest telephone box. It lay in a cluster of back-to-back terraced houses that sprawled under the viaduct carrying the lines between London Road and Oxford Road railway stations.

The sound of children playing their street games brought a smile to Clayton's lips, the chants and verses unchanged since the days when he was a lad. A ball landed at his feet; the toe of his boot stopped it, he looked at the boys and kicked it back. They took up their game and disappeared down a wide cobbled alley. When he reached Keith Street he scanned to see which homes had lights on and which did not;

three houses stood in darkness. Choosing a well-lit house with polished step and gloss painted door he gave the brass knocker a tap.

The lady of the house welcomed him in and once inside, closed the door.

A fire burned merrily, its flames reflecting in the polished brasses placed around the hearth. Clayton beamed, the smell of furniture polish, bringing memories of his grandmother. The man sat by the fire gave a grunt, turned the page of his newspaper and continued to read.

Clayton put his warrant badge away. 'I'm making enquiries about the lady who died a year ago and lived with her nephew here, in this street.'

'Do you mean David and Ethel?'

'Yes, I've learned the will's been settled in David's favour.'

She let out a sigh. 'Thank goodness for that. Did you hear Godfrey? They've sorted it out at last for David.'

Godfrey ruffled his paper, 's'got nowt to do with us, Edna.'

Embarrassed by the husband's rudeness Edna lowered her voice, 'Oh don't mind him, he's not been right since he retired. Personally, I think it's cruel to push folk out of work just because they're old. She plumped the cushions on the sofa, 'Sit down Inspector, would you like a cup of tea?'

'No thank you Mrs...?'

'Carrington. You know really, you should be calling on Dorothy at number 62, she's David's aunty. Oh but wait, they'll not be back from Birmingham. Here Godfrey, when did Stan say they'd be back?'

Irritated, her husband put his paper down. 'I've told yer Edna, s'got nowt t'do with us, David's 'ad enough trouble wi'coppers as it is.'

Sensing it was time to leave, Clayton turned towards the door, noting the look of sympathy from Edna. 'Thank you Mrs Carrington.'

Away from the disapproving looks of her husband, Edna stepped onto the pavement closing her door to. 'I'm sorry about Godfrey. He knows not all policemen are bad. I know you haven't come to harm David. Anyway, he's not moved back yet.' She nodded directly across the street to a house without lights.

'Goodnight Mrs Carrington, and get back to that fire before the cold creeps in.'

Only when she'd watched the nice young policeman turn the corner at the end of the street did Edna re-enter her home and close the door.

Clayton ran to the alleyway and counted each house until he reached the rear of the one pointed out by Edna. Curtains were pulled across the back windows but between the pelmet and track, chinks of light escaped, highlighting the fabric's folds. There was someone at home in dead Aunty Ethel's house.

He ran on and came out of the entry by the viaduct. He needed back-up, needed someone who could handle the situation with care. Dean was right, MacLean wasn't stupid, and he'd spun a web of untruths from the start. Headlights from a car parked under the bridge flashed, Clayton looked across and the driver beckoned. When he approached, the window on the driver's side rolled down and a wiry haired head with matching moustache poked out.

'Good evening Detective Inspector Clayton, I presume we're on the same trail. Would you like a ham sandwich?'

133

JOHNSON PLACED the diversion barrier across the blocked-off lane and fastened it tight against the fence. The road construction workers had finished for the day, their heavy machinery parked up by the curb. Jenkins joined him.

'All done?'

Johnson nodded.

'Come on, it's not that bad.'

'Not that bad? Early starts, late finishes – no paid overtime, who're you kiddin?' Johnson nudged the sandbag into place with his foot; soggy grit oozed over his black polished boots, he swore and marched towards the van.

'Look,' said Jenkins, running to catch up. 'I just picked 'em up, put 'em in me pocket and forgot. It was pissing down. We had to clear the road. Anyway the kids had vanished by then. We weren't to know.'

Johnson turned onto his colleague. 'I shoved Sharples off the road - 'e fell down, I thought 'e was nowt but a ghoul. But 'e was right all along. If you'd've shown me the keys, I'd've taken 'im seriously an' *we* wouldn't be in this hell-hole.'

'Aye, you're not wrong there.' They turned towards the voice; Barry Brocklehurst stepped into the light: behind him three more officers. 'Did Wilson show up?'

Johnson shook his head. 'Why should he?'

'Thought he might've that's all.' Brocklehurst opened his palm. ''And over the van keys Johnson.'

'Why?'

'Chief Superintendent Fisher wants a word,' the burley Sergeant turned his attention to Jenkins, 'and you Jenkins, he especially wants a word with *you.*'

'FAULKNER, CHARLIE Faulkner,' the thin pale hand grasped Clayton's with surprising strength. 'I've got a flask of hot tea.' He twinkled.

'I'm sorry – but there's something I…'

Charlie shook his head. 'No there isn't and who can you trust anyway?'

'I beg your pardon?'

'Granted. Now please – get into the car – its freezing.'

Clayton gave Faulkner a frown, crossed to the passenger side and got in.

'I was wondering when someone from Lever Street was going to get something right at last.' Charlie handed a white paper bag to Clayton; the aroma of ham leaked from it. Clayton's stomach gave a gurgle. 'Freshly made,' said Charlie pointing to a corner shop beside the viaduct.

Steam filmed the windscreen opaque when hot tea poured into a plastic cup was passed to Clayton. Finding another cup under the dash, Charlie blew bits out of it and poured a drink for himself.

'Yes,' said Faulkner taking a sip of the scalding tea, 'I was beginning to think nobody with any brain was looking for them.' He looked into Clayton's eyes, ' He's got the girls in there,'

Clayton wiped his side of the windscreen, when it cleared he had a good view of Aunty Ethel's house. 'He must have them tied up,' he whispered suddenly afraid for them. He placed the cup on the floor and made a move to open the passenger door.

'Don't let the cold in,' cried Faulkner, 'he's not tied them up.

'But he's got the girls in there?'

'Yes – it isn't MacLean the children fear – it's…'

A loud rap hit the fogged up window on Faulkner's side. He wound it down. A dirty-faced lad stood in the road. He brandished half a crown. 'Girl at the bus-stop ses to give yer this,' he shoved a note onto Charlie's lap and ran off.

'What girl?' shouted Clayton, already climbing out of the car and heading where the boy had indicated.

'Dunno,' the lad called back – flicking the coin into the air and catching it. 'Never seen 'em afore or their Dad.'

DROPPED OFF by Faulkner, Clayton ran through the group of photographer's blocking the steps and looked around for B.B. Not able to find him he ran to his own office, where he hoped to find Parker or any other policeman he could trust. Stood in Hammond's office was Superintendent Patterson; who turned and walked to greet the Detective Inspector.

'Good evening Clayton,' he held out his hand. 'I've been seconded for the foreseeable future.'

Delighted Clayton took the offered hand. 'Very pleased Sir, I've traced the missing children.' Preventing Patterson from jumping to conclusions Clayton held both hands in front. 'But unfortunately, they've left and are on the move.'

Omitting Whiteman and the flat in his factory from the story, Clayton told Patterson everything he'd learned about MacLean. They drove to Keith Street. With them were Davies and Constable Brown.

'I'm certain he means no harm to the children,' said Clayton, Dean's words echoing inside his head. 'He's babysat for the Depot's personnel. They can vouch for him.'

'No Clayton, I disagree; if that man intended no harm he'd have handed them into the protection of the court.'

'With respect Sir, they lived in fear of authority. Maybe MacLean knows that, he's certainly aware of Wilson's brutality.'

Patterson sunk back into the leather. 'You think he's protecting the children from their father.'

'Yes.'

'What will he do?'

Clayton paused before he answered, 'I think he'll make us believe he's heading for Yorkshire, the children's grandmother perhaps. He'll hope that'll draw Wilson too.'

'Whilst he takes the children to safety?'

They pulled up outside Aunty Ethel's front door. Patterson stepped out, walked to greet the driver of the vehicle behind and gave instructions. He turned to Clayton. 'Don't worry Detective Inspector there'll be no ripping it apart. I just want forensic to give the place a going over before we spread our dabs everywhere.'

THE GREY Flamingo's main bar was open for members only. It advertised happy hour – discounted drinks devised to grab early evening trade from the city's pubs. Alfredo sat at the end of the bar surrounded by a few regulars. Elsewhere, people sat in cosy alcoves where they sipped half price cocktails, listened to the resident pianist and spoke in low, hushed tones.

Wilson barged in – followed by Harry, the nightclub's bouncer.

Customers looked to Alfredo, his story halted mid-sentence and sensing danger drank up, gathered their belongings, and prepared to leave.

'And since when has it been acceptable to gate-crash my brother's bar?' Alfredo roared, looking to Harry for an answer.

'Sorry Mr Boss, 'e pushed past.' Harry went to grab the intruder. Wilson shrugged him off, moved towards the bar.

'Your brother has something for me. Hammond arranged it.'

Frowning, Alfredo kept his attention on Harry, 'Who's the creep?'

Wilson grabbed Alfredo's sleeve, around the room people moved from their tables and filed into the foyer. Those sat around the bar slunk away and followed. Alfredo rose from the barstool towering Wilson and grabbed the policeman's coat front.

'I told you. Hammond arranged it.' Wilson said. Undaunted by the gangster's height, he tried to break free. Alfredo held him at arm's length and continued to address Harry.

'What's he talkin' about?'

'Could be the fella Jim mentioned, but e's too early. Bernardo told 'im to come tomorrow.'

Alfredo turned to Wilson. 'Not the first time I've looked into those mad eyes is it?' He turned back to address the bouncer. 'Who is he?'

'Don't talk as though I'm not in the room.' Wilson snarled, grabbing hold of the outstretch sleeve, trying to free his coat from Alfredo's iron grip. The crunch to his nose came so hard and fast it sent Wilson across the room, crashing him into a cluster of recently vacated chairs.

Alfredo smoothed the creases from his sleeve and reached for his cigar, 'Like I said Harry, who the fuck is he?'

BY THE time the Land Rover had crossed the Pennines and reached the Lancashire mill town of Oldham, snow was falling thick and fast. The Openshaw brothers filled the petrol tank, ate fish and chips and pressed on reaching a shabby inner-city bed and breakfast hotel before nine and booked in. Leaving his brother to tend to his pigeons, Josh strolled round to meet with Reggie Spencer, a convicted paedophile and fellow inmate recently released after serving three years for sex crimes. They agreed on a plan to lure Mike Wilson using children enticed by Spencer that bore a resemblance to Audrey and Linda.

News that Josh and Jake's mother had contacted the police came too late to be included in the evening papers. But the radio in the hotel's sitting room ran a worrying news item. It told of a released child molester, once captured by Sergeant Wilson and now claiming to have knowledge of the whereabouts of the missing children. Josh Openshaw's mother, the announcer said, is sick with worry – saying prison had turned her son's mind – made him into a pervert. She begged the police to find her son before he reached the little girls.

Josh smiled at the news – searched for his brother and took him on a tour of the city.

CHAPTER ELEVEN

ALFREDO BOSS put the telephone back onto its cradle and drew on his cigar. Lazily, his eyes studied the guy sprawled across the floor – blood pouring from his nostrils.

'Why didn't you say that you were the Wilson who used to hang around with Hammond in the good old days?' He reached across the bar, grabbed a teacloth and threw it to Wilson. 'Here, wipe your nose before you bloody my brother's carpet.' He strolled to the entrance lobby, 'Harry, while I take our friend into Jim's office – you get those punters back. Offer a free drink. And Joe,' he called to the pianist, 'play somethin' for our uninvited guest.' He stood and assessed Wilson's state, 'His requested choice would be … *friendless and blue*.'

Whilst the ivories picked up the melody of '*I'll get along somehow*', Alfredo ushered Wilson into the manager's office and closed the door. The click of the automatic locking device sent shivers down Wilson's spine – he was trapped – trapped with a bloody gangster at that. Tilting his head to stem the flow of blood he caught sight of the dance floor below and the lonely figure of the pianist playing under the spotlight. The tinkle wafted up through the office window reminding Wilson of happier days. Days when he and Kathleen held each other close and danced the night away.

From the rear of the club, someone approached the piano and slapped the player's raised palm en route to the bar. The ease with which the man addressed those around him informed Wilson it was *his* office they stood in. Jim Whittaker had been briefed of Wilson's premature appearance and came prepared to accommodate the wishes of his employer, Bernardo Boss. The automatic lock clicked open; Whittaker entered the room paying scant attention to the sorry looking policeman to address Alfredo.

'I'm not surprised Hammond wants this idiot shifted abroad. His mug's plastered all over the front pages.' He tossed his car keys onto the desk together with a small paper package before turning to Wilson. 'That swollen conk might be to your advantage – you'll need all the edge you can muster when going through customs. Don't rely too much on this passport because it won't take close scrutiny, it had to be rushed.' He nudged the package towards Wilson, who opened it, flicking through the contents. Whittaker turned to the safe, took out a batch of notes and split off a portion. 'Bernardo says to give him five hundred quid. It's to be taken out of Hammond's account.' Alfredo nodded, Whittaker placed the remainder of the cash back in the safe and continued to address Wilson, There's a passage booked on a ship leaving for Malta tomorrow evening. Pick the ticket up at Furness, Crane's office tomorrow afternoon.'

'No!' Wilson blurted, 'the game's up with them. Hammond told me.'

Alarm spread in Alfredo's eyes, he reached for the phone Whittaker reassured saying, 'There's nothing about Furness Crane in the papers. Honestly Alfredo, the only news is about some missing kids being traced to Yorkshire.' Alfredo continued to dial whilst Whittaker looked at Wilson,

'They're sayin' they're your kids and that deaf guy took 'em. Y'know, the one you had in the cells then set free.'

Wilson's wit rallied, *MacLean*? While his brain raced his eyes took in the two men holding him prisoner – their mind now on other matters. He placed the documents back inside the envelope, palmed the car keys and stood up. 'What time did you say for the tickets?'

Whittaker replied whilst reaching for the lock release on the door. 'Two – they said to call after lunch.' Wilson nodded, tossed the blooded cloth onto the desk and left the Grey Flamingo nightclub.

FLURRIES OF snow settled on the shoulders of Detective Inspector Clayton's overcoat as he walked along the station's platform in time to catch the mail train to Leeds. After much persuasion, Superintendent Patterson relented, allowing Clayton to visit Kathleen's mother in Leeds, mostly with the hope of tricking Wilson to follow. Arrangements had been made for officers of Filey Road Police Station in Leeds to meet Clayton and escort him to the home of Mary Williams.

WILSON RAN a hand over the dashboard. Polished walnut: Jim Whittaker had taste. He pulled out of the car park and slid silently eastward along the back streets. Frozen snow stuck to the windscreen, he fumbled for the wiper switch, his fingers clumsy with unfamiliarity until they sensed the button and flicked the blades into action. Snow came down in shilling size flakes, but the warm air of the dash kept his screen clear. He tried to relax – work out how he was going to get to MacLean before anyone else.

He was sick of having a blood-encrusted nose. It irritated and with each intake of breath, it sent pangs of pain across his cheekbones – bloody gangsters – Greeks, Italians, they're all the bloody same. His life was in ruins, his wife dead, kids in the hands of a pervert, lodgings and car crawling with police and the lump on the back of his head the size of a golf ball throbbed with renewed gusto.

As he sped out of town the engine of the XK150 purred a gentle rhythm. Inside Wilson's head, the throbbing eased making way for more melodic pitches and the tinkle of ivory keys tapped out a tune. Further along the road, cars were being urged to slow down, he swallowed as caped officers came into view and swerved as the car in front clamped on the brakes too soon: his Ronson lighter slid off the passenger seat and onto the floor, out of reach. Wilson cursed; but his immediate concentration was on the police ahead. He strained his eyes to see what was amiss before realising Belle Vue's crowds were leaving the stadium.

The police were simply controlling pedestrians and the traffic. He breathed his relief in a lengthy sigh, 'Mike me ol' mate, you're losing your nerve.' Slowly he passed by the policemen, their attention focused on keeping the traffic flowing and dispersing the crowds. He and Johnson shared crowd duty in the good old days. In the good old days when he and Johnson were best of mates, before bloody Jenkins and bloody Hammond came on the scene. Fuck 'em. He turned left keeping a diagonal route towards the higher lands in the direction of the Pennines. He reached for a cigarette pulled one clear of the packet and fumbled for the car's cigar lighter. He missed the button and lost his path momentarily before realising his mistake and turning the headlights on again. Nice motor, he smiled, just got to get used to her.

Once he could feel the kick of nicotine, Wilson settled into the car's leather seat and allowed his mental pianist to take up residence inside his head and play the music again. It tinkled *friendless and blue* over in his mind, his brain calming until a clod of snow gathered in the corner of the screen and slid loose blocking his view. Immediately he cursed – slamming a fist onto the steering wheel before the return blade automatically swept the clod away, his action cut off the soothing music, bringing instead the pulse of pain, beating like a tom-tom driving him insane.

SNOW, FALLING thick and fast hampered the driver's way. Gritters were out in force but only on the major roads. Having introduced Clayton to the elderly woman, the driver promised to return in the appointed hour's time and left.

Clayton took off his overcoat, placed it on a dining chair back and sat in the seat offered. 'I am sorry to call at such a late hour Mrs Williams, but the news I carry is not good.'

'If you've come to tell me Kathleen's been assaulted again, I'm not interested.' Her wrinkled face set ready for conflict.

'No, I've come to tell you Kathleen is dead. She was knocked down by a car.' Shocked by his own bluntness Clayton added, 'I'm very sorry, is there someone we could get to stay with you?'

The face opposite him remained hard, lips thin and tight; the eyes clear blue, pupils hard as jet. She used them to study Clayton. 'There's no need to be bothering folks at this time of night. What 'appened?'

'She was crossing the road during the rush hour.'

'You're not from these parts? Where was it?'

'Manchester.'

Her features flashed with disbelief. 'What the 'ell was she doing in Manchester?' before Clayton could reply, she narrowed her eyes, 'who drove the car – was it Michael Wilson?'

'No – a lady driver skidded on the wet surface – she's receiving hospital treatment for her injuries – but your daughter, unfortunately never regained consciousness.'

'Uhh! But I'll warrant 'e'll not've bin far away.'

The canny old lady wasn't wrong there – Clayton learnt Wilson was in Manchester that night. 'Mrs Williams, I need you to tell me about David MacLean.'

The cold eyes suddenly lost their focus. 'Why?'

'Have you read any of the papers?'

'Waste of time ' nowt but lies in 'em'

'David may try to reach you.'

'Can't think why – there's nowt for 'im 'ere – unless the rest of the family's fleeced 'im an' 'e's penniless.'

'He isn't penniless Mrs Williams, but he may have something for you.'

Her eyes widened. 'What?'

'Two little girls.'

She scowled: clearly the children had not entered her mind. 'Well 'e can bugger off. I'm too old for this.' Then by way of explanation, 'Doesn't the twit know that Mike'll find 'em an' then we'll all feel 'is wrath?' She straightened the tablecloth in front of her, rose without difficulty and nodded towards Clayton's coat. 'You'd better catch up with yon driver Inspector, 'ave 'eard all I want. I'll bid yer goodnight.'

With a slow nod, Clayton remained seated, picked up his notebook and placed it inside his jacket pocket. 'Before I leave Mrs Williams, there's a man called Joshua Openshaw who served time for interfering with children here in Leeds. Mike Wilson was the arresting officer. Would he know where Audrey and Linda are?

145

'Can't see why – the family are known around 'ere. Folks say it were a trumped up charge. Josh's dad campaigned relentlessly for 'is release. Cost 'im dear in the end – damaged 'is 'ealth an' killed the poor man.'

'So Joshua Openshaw is out for revenge against Wilson?

'Josh'll 'ave ter join the queue; Mike's gathered plenty of enemies without 'im.' A feint smile crossed her lips, 'We'd not be so lucky Inspector. Mike's one of those folk who gets away with murder. 'E's 'ard as nails and nowt'll stop 'im, least of all Josh Openshaw.'

Clayton nodded, but remained seated. 'Then tell me Mrs Williams, does David know enough about your family, enough *not* to bring the children to Leeds?'

'Can't say, unless Kathleen told 'im about Mike. But if she didn't – then bloody know-it-all Audrey would put 'im right.' Contempt in her manner displayed actual dislike for the child.

He rose. 'It was just a thought, you being their grandmother. But, well sorry to have disturbed you.' Disappointed he'd learned nothing Clayton left the mental fishing rod to dangle at the edge of his sea of detection and tried another tactic. He inclined his head to photographs pinned around the sitting room wall.

'You do have other grandchildren then?'

Eyes warming a degree rested on the photo Clayton eyed. 'Oh yes,' she beamed. 'That's our Benny.' A chubby faced boy with missing front teeth grinned at the camera. 'An' that's our Peter, can swim the length of the baths – got a badge to prove it.' Clayton stared at the old lady's transformation.

'My granny always denied she loved us boys best – but our Liz knew she favoured us.'

146

'S'got nowt to do with favouritism.' She snapped, 'these children 'ave a proper dad. Our Tom's a wonderful father – and a good 'usband to 'is wife.' She sneered showing gleaming plastic teeth. ''Ave you any idea what it's like to see your daughter beaten, time and time again?'

Lost for a reply Clayton shook his head.

'No, I didn't think so. We pleaded with 'er to give 'im up. But no – silly sod thought 'e could be cured. Mike wrecked 'is own 'ome and wrecked ours when we sheltered 'er.' She sat down – wrung her bony hands as though washing them. 'The last time I saw Kathleen was April, at the get together. Wasn't much cop. Kathleen looked awful, she'd learnt nowt over the years – stupid sod had 'ad Linda since last I knew.'

'The get together?' Echoes of Mr Dean's statement came to the fore causing the line to twitch, was there a nibble?

She pushed back the waves in her hair, patting them into place before resuming the cleansing of her hands. 'It was our Dorothy's idea. With Ethel gone she was keen to unite the family. A mistake, I think the past is well left alone, don't you?'

'Yes, I do,' he lied.

A wicked smile lit her eyes. 'Why, you got a few skeletons?'

Clayton returned the smile, showing his dimples, 'I'd be thankful for a bit of a life Mrs Williams, but there are things better kept buried.'

She nodded, clasped her bony fingers, resting them on top of the snow-white tablecloth. 'In my youth I got into trouble and Ethel took me in. After the baby's birth it was clear 'e wasn't right. I was in no fit state to rear a baby let alone a daft one, so I arranged for it to be 'ospitalised.' She looked straight into Clayton's eyes, 'I'm not proud of what I did. Anyway Ethel insisted she'd care for it,' she pressed unseen creases out of the tablecloth, 'she doted on the scraggy little thing, so I agreed to leave her to it. Next I saw of 'im was at the reunion – all grown up but just as stupid, deaf and dumb with it.'

'Did the whole family attend the re-union?'

'Oh yes, but our end found David difficult. Mind you, Kathleen got on with 'im but she's 'ad plenty of practise with nutters, married one for a start.'

Clayton gestured to the photos. 'And the boys? Did they get on well with the rest of the family?' He gave the rod's reel a bit of a turn.

'Nah! Like I said, David's hard work. We got Kathleen's girls to swap seats. That way we could be on our own.'

'Did the girls not mind David?'

'Oh no, they also got on like 'ouse on fire.'

'Tell me Mrs Williams, is there any chance David has seen Mike Wilson in the past?'

She shook her head. 'Can't 'ave, Dorothy only arranged the reunion in April. Kathleen was still on the run from Mike – very nearly didn't mek it accordin' to our Dot.'

Clayton was reminded of Whiteman's comment about her having to cut and run at a moment's notice. 'It's just he wrote something about Mike, like he knew he was a sergeant in uniform?'

'Unless 'e's seen wedding photo – Mike wore 'is uniform: our Dorothy was sent a copy.'

'Aye that'll be it – and it's unlikely they'll come to you?'

The old lady gave sigh, got up from her chair once more. 'No, David won't come 'ere. There's nowt for any of 'em. An' they know they're not wanted.'

'Yes, you've made that very clear Mrs Williams.' He held open his coat ready to put it on. 'I came to inform you of Kathleen's death and also, to enquire into the likelihood of David bringing the children to you.'

'Why didn't yer ask 'im? I know 'e's dumb but I've seen 'im write things down.' She focused on him. 'What's wrong?'

'David lied – he's taken the children and it's being treated as abduction. He's in serious trouble.'

'Abduction? Oh come off it – the lad 'asn't the nous to wipe 'is arse properly. David's not abducted those girls. If anything, they've kidnapped 'im. It'll be that bloody Audrey. I tell yer Inspector she's a canny little madam, she'll be behind it.'

'We think David's trying to protect them from their father.'

She laughed, genuine – as though Clayton had said something really amusing. 'Yer can't protect summat from Mike – he's crazy. And David's dafter than I thought if 'e thinks 'e can.' She shook her head. 'No, the brains behind any abduction will be Audrey's. She'll be protecting Linda from Mike's rage.'

'Why? What has Linda to do with this?'

Her bony shoulders gave a shrug. 'I don't know. But I watched how Audrey looked after her sister, mentioned it to Kathleen, but she wouldn't open up. My feelin' is Mike's done something bad – something either to Linda or Audrey. They'll not allow him to do it again, of that, I'm positive.'

'Could Linda be another man's child?'

The plastic smile again. 'Never – that's the tragedy of it – she only 'ad eyes for Mike.'

Clayton pulled up his collar and dragged in his puny catch. 'Sorry to have asked – but I'm trying to find where Mike's rage is rooted.'

'Mike doesn't need a reason – 'e's mad an' that's an end to it.' Suddenly focussed, the old lady reached towards Clayton. 'You shouldn't 'ave come 'ere – Mike'll think yer onto summat and follow. I don't want 'im coming 'ere. Quick, get yer driver to tek me up to our Tom's place.'

THE BLURRED image of the lusty blonde looked back from every angle, surrounding Hammond with a haze of black crepe chiffon and dazzling diamonds, 'you li'le temtressh,' he saluted. The image returned his leer with a lob-sided smile, beckoning him to come closer. Shades of pink brushed down from the ceiling, the satin bedspread aglow in the bedroom's muted light. Hips swaying he ventured forward, eyes fixed on the sultry blonde. He kicked off his shoes where they fell amongst others worn than night. In the outer room, the music ended abruptly leaving a void to be filled by frozen rain hitting hard against the window. Hammond moved the thick curtain aside and peered down. Another world lay behind the glass, a stark one in a wintry swirl, bare trees laden with thick snow, black against the white, falling fast and thick – in its midst, the ghost of an overweight man dressed as a tart looked back. With a shudder, he let go of the drape, drained his glass and staggered out of the room.

He needed to dispel the window's image from his mind. He stopped by the bathroom door where the light fell softer, his reflection bearable, bathing it with kindness, even glamour. Hammond's spirits rose, he smiled again, sinking his silk stockinged toes into the plush pile, the feeling sensual and arousing. He turned towards the record player, placed his glass on the side table and set the music to play. He was going to have a party. A ball! And all the worries of the past months were to disappear; to be left behind with his boring suit and plain little Austin car parked up by the glove factory. When, if – they find it, he surmised, they'd never connect Hammond with the nice lady who parked her Riley in a garage three blocks away.

Music on full volume he drained the bottle into his glass and returned to the bedroom for the climax of the evening.

The image never failed to delight. He ran manicured hands over the bedspread, finding the silk scarfs by touch. The stirring thrilled, it was positively insatiable! How many times? Filthy beast!

Eyes flickered to the bedpost, to the handcuff hanging free, waiting to lock his wrist. Then to the foot of the bed where more silk ribbons were tied – waiting to trap ankles stretching legs taut and wide apart. It was time. All the fooling earlier mere foreplay meant to tickle and whet the appetite for the grand banquet – the feast of delight too good to be shared.

JIM WHITTAKER replaced the phone on the cradle and swore out loud at his own stupidity. How could he allow his pride and joy, his Jaguar to be stolen from under his nose? And snatched by nothing but a tow-rag of a copper. Following the information gathered, Wilson could be heading for Leeds. Leeds may be a place the policeman knew well, but Whittaker knew nothing was certain with the manic state the man was in. He took a deep breath and put his trust into Barry to cut him off before he reached the Pennines.

BARRY JONES reached the crest of the tor, pulled onto the filling station's car park, and turned the Land Rover round facing the way he'd come. He flicked off his lights and watched the snow cover his tracks. Reaching for the jackets, Barry passed one to his partner and slid his arms into his own. Down below: the road twisted into the distance, the lights of a snowplough illuminating the scene as it moved slow but sure and steady pushing piles of dirty snow into ditches along its path. Barry's companion handed him a flask, he took a swig and gave it back. 'We've made good time,' Barry said eyes never leaving the snowplough's progress.

'What about the shipment?'

'Pick it up on the way back – Jim wants his Jag, we were in the area, so to speak. Now fasten your jacket, keep your eyes peeled and wait.'

The plough's red taillights disappeared behind the dark hulk of the hillside. Seconds ticked by with breath-holding slowness before it re-appeared. It lumbered towards the crossroads turned to face uphill and began to climb. Barry sat up – eyes fixed further down the track and locked onto the headlights of a lone vehicle, it too disappeared momentarily when another hill blanked it out. The snowplough, now with headlights facing, trudged up the winding road, the lone car was travelling at speed, closing the distance between them. Barry gave the throttle a push, the Rover's engine growled obediently, ready for action. The snowplough reached the hill and disappeared behind it, followed closely by the car on its tail.

'The stupid bugger's going too fast.' Barry's companion cried. They prepared to intercept the moment the Jaguar was spotted. Lights ablaze and engine roaring, Barry re-joined the twisting road and headed upwards to the point where traffic could be halted.

IN A brief moment of lucidity, Wilson's mind began to clear. Is this what he'd come down to – stealing cars? Mike Wilson: the scourge of deviants – pride of the force – a car thief. A memory leapt in – one with mates congratulating him – they'd had a whip-round – the gift of a Ronson lighter. All long ago, in a time when he and Kathleen were happy and he never felt the deep emptiness now aching through his chest. What happened? Did life begin to break down when the liberal minded voiced their concerns about his tactics? What tactics? He'd caught sex offenders in the act – or about to act – and nabbed them: fair and simple. What did liberals know about perverts? Had they been at the receiving end? No. And now those same liberals had let MacLean go – if they'd only listened; Sharples would've been okay. He groaned as another memory leapt in uninvited – the doll mender bent double in his own hallway.

The car sped on, tyres gripping the snow, lapping up the miles as the road spread out before him. He should turn back – leave the Jaguar where Whittaker could find it; lie low before picking the ticket for Malta – escape from all this shit. Nice idea, but what of the girls? Good question - what of them? If the truth were known – they're better off without him. That bumbling Clayton fella would find them eventually – place them in care where they'd be safe. Safe in care – never.

Under the reins of its manic driver the Jaguar purred on and reached the high ground of the lower Pennine Chain. Ahead: the crossroad where direction signs were unreadable, coated with wind-driven snow but Wilson needed no indication to mark the way. Having traversed these roads many times he pointed the pussycat's nose up the incline and rounded the bend. What dreams did Kathleen have for the girls? What chance did they ever have while running from one filthy slum to another? He'd failed her – failed them. He should turn the car round, take the opportunity to start afresh; then when the time was right – take the girls to a better life.

He remembered that a service station lay ahead, could almost taste the meat filled pies they served and made a mental note to call in. Under the pressure of Wilson's foot, the Jaguar's throttle increased the speed as it rounded the hill's curve. His fingers found the cigarette pack, pulled one out and placed it between his cracked lips. Ahead, another bend disappeared behind a dark, looming hill: Wilson maintained the speed, reached for the dash's cigar lighter and was plunged into total darkness.

When he corrected the mistake it was too late. The headlights no longer held the road ahead but pointed across a wilderness of craggy rocks and snowdrifts. The nearside wheel dipped off the road taking the rest of the car over the edge. It lurched from rock to boulder knocking Wilson from his seat before finally coming to a stop.

BARRY JONES pulled the Land Rover over, wound down his window and yelled for the driver to halt. Mistaking Barry's uniform jacket for officers of mountain rescue, the snowplough driver did as commanded. Any second now, Barry presumed, the Jaguar would round the bend and be forced to brake. He and Johnny were ready. Ready for any resistance the policeman might put up. They waited.

''Owt wrong?' asked the plough driver.

'Yeh – speedin' vehicle on your tail – where did it go?'

The ploughman shrugged his shoulders and muttered. 'Bin nowt on roads since tea – reckon folk's got better things t'do in weather like this.'

'Aye – 'appen you're right – but we saw a car head round this hill. Stay put – keep yer lights on full while I take a look.' He turned to his partner. 'Move over Johnny – keep the engine warm and be ready to stop Wilson getting through. I think he's pulled a fast one.'

'What about other road users? Am I to let 'em through?

'Not yet – let me find Wilson first.' He pulled the fur-lined hood tight around his face, switched on his torch and headed into the swirling freezing blizzard.

WILSON MOVED his neck – grinding grizzle crunched inside his ears, something hard and painful dug into his skull. He opened his eyes and listened. The Jaguar's wheels were spinning. Was the engine still running? When he raised his shoulders, his brain swooned – no – his mind urged – this is no place to conk out. The car was on its side – the driver's door beneath him. He sniffed the air – petrol, shit, he tried to pitch his ears above the outside gale, listen if the engine was running: *fire* his mind warned - he had to get out. His head swimming, he used the seats to leaver his body straight, tried the passenger door handle above him and pushed. 'Jesus,' it didn't budge. He felt for the window opener and as he wound it across gravel, rocks and scree fell into the car – wetting his collar and trickling down his back. He scrambled up the leather upholstery and pushed through the open gap.

The car had come to rest in a ditch. One headlight smashed, the other under snow. It gave off an eerie sheen. Unbelievable to Wilson, the engine hummed – unsteady, and missing the odd beat – but the pussycat hummed. She's going to burst into flames warned Wilson's brain.

Obeying instinct he crawled through the snow and kept on crawling to put as much distance between himself and the crumpled whiskers of Jim Whittaker's pride and joy.

CHAPTER TWELVE

CLAYTON WAS surprised to see Superintendent Patterson at work in Hammond's old office. It was 7.15am Hammond never arrived before eight.

'Good morning Clayton,' the Superintendent hailed, 'good trip?'

'Mornin' Sir – didn't get as much info as I would've liked. But this might be interesting.' He pulled a large envelope out of his inside pocket, handed it to Patterson before taking off his overcoat and hanging it up. 'Superintendent Hitchins from Filey Road gathered it for me. It's information about Joshua Openshaw.'

Patterson cleared a place on his desk, spread the documents out and began to read. 'Has Davies arrived?' he asked without looking up.

Clayton checked his watch, 'Be here any moment.' He strolled to the corner sink, filled the kettle and plugged it in. 'Cuppa tea Sir?' Patterson nodded engrossed in the data sent by Hitchins.

Davies came in with O'Brien followed by a bleary-eyed Parker. In silence they took off their coats and made for their individual desks. Clayton picked up a new cup, looked across to Davies who nodded towards Patterson's office.

There were six brand new mugs on the drainer. Things were looking up.

'Very interesting,' Patterson said turning to the last page. Clayton joined him leaving Davies to see to the brew.

'Openshaw doesn't fit the bill does he?'

'No – and the circumstances he was charged with – attempt, not actual.' Patterson closed the file. 'No wonder he's bitter.'

'He volunteered himself to Wilson – actually walked into the station and gave a statement.' Clayton moved aside to allow Davies to put the steaming mugs down. 'Why did he get six years?'

'Four – he served four years.'

'Even so, it's a hell of chunk in anyone's life.'

'Openshaw put it to good use.' Patterson sipped the hot tea. 'As Hitchins reports, the Governor refers to him as a 'model prisoner'. Did you get far with the victim's mother?'

Clayton filled him in.

'We're manning the ports and posted descriptions of Wilson, MacLean, the children and now Openshaw.' Patterson studied Clayton, reached for the telephone and started to dial. 'I'm arranging for you to go home – get some sleep.

'But Sir, I slept on the train.'

'Yes, I can see.'

Was this a touch of Hammond? Was he about to be told he needed a shave? He ran a hand over his whiskers. 'But Sir, this, er Joshua Openshaw,' Clayton urged, 'he needs to be found, he's after revenge. These newspaper articles – they're designed to draw Wilson to him.'

'Leave that to uniform, you go home – like I said get some decent kip and in case it slipped your mind, you're going to the dogs.'

He *is* getting personal.

'The dogs – Brocklehurst says not to be late. The coach leaves outside here at six o'clock prompt.'

DAVID MACLEAN pulled the woollen hat down to his brows and faced the bitter wind. Despite the weather conditions, the boat was scheduled to leave on time. He gripped the suitcase and edged his way up the queue. He'd been lucky so far but it couldn't last. Running around him, a dirty-faced boy chased his little sister. As they neared the gateway, the little girl slipped and whimpered to be picked up. MacLean put down the case, gathered her into his arms where she clung to him, face buried into his neck screaming her heart out. The little boy dragged the case forward, showed the guard the tickets and listened above his sister's racket to where they must go.

The crossing was rough; the prow of the ship dipping deep into the trough of water; washing grey surf over the deck. Most of the passengers were inside. They watched through portholes as the boy and his sister ran to face the force of the spray. They watched as the children turned towards their daddy squealing with delight as foam cascaded from behind. MacLean sat on the slatted wooden seats and mulled over the past hectic days.

What had he done? According to the newspapers he was a pervert. A sexual deviant fit only for castration or worse. He stared at the children. Did they look like the victims of kidnapping? Linda caught his stare, ran towards him and slipped on the wet decking, but Audrey, quick as a dart steadied her fall. The little girl burst into laughter, pink gums above tiny pearls of teeth. She leaned against the boy, braced between his shoe-polish blackened knees and mouthed, 'I'm alright – I'm alright.'

And she was, Linda had weathered the experience better than Audrey. Neither knew yet of the mother's death. MacLean would find a suitable time to tell them. He rubbed his eyes; when that time would be, he didn't know. The ship's prow rose into the gunmetal grey clouds, made another lunge forward and hit the wall of foaming grey water just as the children reached the rail – they turned, hands clasped together and ran, eyes wide towards him. He gave them a weak smile – pretending he too was having fun.

What an extraordinary little girl Audrey had proved to be. He would never have pulled it off without her cunning. And his old school uniform – kept by his sentimental aunty and now used to disguise Audrey as a boy. MacLean stared in admiration. He watched how they played their childish game, yet when the occasion rose, Audrey would be ready to play a different role – that of his ears and mouth. Kathleen had trained them well – for Audrey never let her guard down.

From below, passengers started to appear, stench of vomit on their breath. David braced himself. The children sensed playtime was over and took their place by his side.

He read Audrey's lips. 'They say there's still no sight of land.' He grimaced wondering what awaited them across the horizon.

FROM THE cover of a snowdrift, Wilson dipped his head beneath the surface as an arc of light lit the rim of his hollowed den. He shivered uncontrollably, clenched his teeth tight for fear their chatter could be heard. In one way he thanked the blizzard as it continued unabated, relentless in the swirling bombardment of snow cover, but on the flip side, the cold was numbing him, lulling him to sleep. He was a survivor, he told himself. The medics had told him so, but this time, he held onto consciousness by a thread. How long had he been in this hole? He had no idea. The breakdown truck had been and gone, the Jaguar had been hoisted from the snowdrift and taken away. Now: wrecked with cold he studied the Land Rover parked by the roadside in the lea of the hill. One man remained with it whilst the other searched the area. Paralysed by the beam of light zigzagging towards him, Wilson had no choice but to wait it out or be caught.

A shout, faint in the clamour of the gale caught his attention. He dared to peer over the edge, someone answered, loud and close by. He ducked below the snow's surface. The man making his way towards Wilson held the torch steady and gave it another sweep. Wilson feared this searcher was in for the long haul, one of those men who never gave up. But another call from the man in the distance halted the torchbearer's sweeping search. Close by, very close by – the man with the torch answered again – with reluctance in his voice, he announced he was giving up the search, he turned and his boots knocked against the sides of Wilson's hole.

He lost his footing and slid down the bank sending his torch to roll ahead of him, out of reach.

Wilson's stopped his shiver, held his breath, ears tuned above the roar of the storm listening and waiting for the man to stand up, regain his balance and press on. In what seemed to be an eternity the man scrambled up the slope towards the light of his torch, grabbed it, got to his feet and trudged in the direction of the waiting Land Rover. Wilson let out a long breath, ducked when the headlights passed on the road above him and waited until its engine noise had faded away. For that precious moment, he was left with nothing but the raging storm.

CHAPTER THIRTEEN

BATHED, SHAVED and well rested, Clayton boarded the coach taking the police social group to Belle Vue greyhound races. He braved the wolf whistles from those not used to seeing him 'scrubbed up' and made his way to the back of the bus.

It dropped them off outside the entrance to The Lake, the pub where Clayton had questioned Alice, the curvy barmaid. Before they filed off the coach, he approached Davies and whispered in his ear. 'There's a call I need to make,' he handed the D.C. a ten shilling note, 'get our beers and one for B.B. I'll be back in fifteen minutes.'

He checked the time, if he got a spurt on, he'd reach the sewing factory in time for the opening of the gates. He wanted to let Whiteman know the situation as far as he knew it. Working on pure instinct, he felt the children were safer with MacLean than the other options open to them.

'But I don't like it.' Whiteman's concern showed in every wrinkle on his brow. 'Why should a man throw away his life for two children he barely knows?'

'I have no answer to that. But he is their mother's half brother and from what I can see, he is all they have.'

'My wife is willing to take them into our home.'

Despite whatever problems the cultural differences could cause, Clayton truly believed Whiteman meant to take Audrey and Linda into his German speaking, Jewish way of life.

'We have to find them first. And we are manning the ports and their descriptions have been sent all over the country. As for your concerns, from what I'm learning, Audrey is more than capable of escaping from MacLean if she wanted to. You know how many times they've picked up sticks and ran. If MacLean has bad intentions, she will act.'

'She's eight years old. I know she has an old head on her shoulders, but she is still a child – a child who likes to play with a doll.' Suddenly remembering, 'How is that poor man, the toy repairer?'

'He'll pull through.' Clayton sighed. 'Which is why I feel the girls are safe with MacLean. What happened to Oliver Sharples was mindless. Such unnecessary violence has to be a sickness. In a way I feel sorry for the perpetrator, surely it was clear that Wilson needed help a long time ago?'

'He got help, but according to Kathleen, Hammond had him signed off the sick and arranged a clean bill of health,' Whiteman went to the safe, brought out the bank passbook. 'What do I do with her savings?'

'Keep everything safe. Whatever happens I'm sure they will contact you sometime.'

'There's this – it's a sort of 'to whom it concerns' kind of letter but it tells us exactly how much Kathleen feared her husband.' Whiteman handed an open hand-written letter to Clayton. 'Reading it, I am sure you are right. Michael Wilson does need specialised medical help.'

'I know.' Clayton read the words. 'This reads like a message from the grave.' He handed it back. 'Keep it with other things. By the way, Hammond's been suspended. We have Patterson in his place.'

'That's the best news I heard in a long time. Would you like a drink or are you expected elsewhere.' Whiteman referred to Clayton's new suit.

'Police social do, we're going to the dogs.'

PATHOLOGIST DR Adrian Crowther tapped his fingers with impatience until eventually, Superintendent Patterson came to the phone: only then did he disclose his findings.

'I thought discretion would be better served if you dealt with this,' he told Patterson, 'I mean to say Lever Street.'

'I understand, I'll have a car sent for D.I. Clayton. Are the roads clear?'

'They were clear enough for me to get through. I'll wait here for Ian.'

CLAYTON MADE his way through the crowded pub; a pint of best bitter was passed above the heads of fellow officers and placed into his hand. He downed half of it in almost one gulp.

'Better get another in,' B.B. called over to Davies, 'man with a thirst here.'

Clayton wiped the froth from his upper lip, gave a wide grin and drank the rest of the pint. 'Bloody gorgeous,' he managed just as Alice glided through the crowd carrying a stack of empty glasses. She steadied the stack on one hip, reached up with her free hand and patted Clayton's cheek.

'Feeling better after the other morning?'

'Much better thank you Alice.'

'Good.' She gave his cheek another gentle tap and continued collecting glasses. Glancing over her shoulder, she saw he followed her with his eyes and gave him a radiant smile.

DAVIES AND Clayton stood in the queue waiting to place their bets. 'So she's not your young lady?'

'No.'

'Not me wants to know Sir, it's the lads, they're putting two and two tog…..'

'I know what they're doing. Tell 'em it's none of their business.'

'Told 'em already, but you know O'Brien, not 'appy until he's got the ins and outs of everything.' Davies stopped talking, stood on tiptoe to stare back along the queue. 'What's Barber doing 'ere?' Davies turned back to Clayton, 'He's spotted us, 'e's coming over.'

'Sorry to interrupt your social night Sir,' Barber addressed Clayton, 'but I've been instructed to be your driver for the evening. Superintendent Patterson's orders, we have to leave straight away.'

CLAYTON STEPPED over the broken glass and stood in the hall.

'Come on up Ian.'

'Thought I recognised the car.' Clayton smiled at hearing the voice of the jovial pathologist. 'What's with all the cloak and dagger stuff?'

He turned the bend on the stairs and caught the cold breeze gushing across the landing. In the room opposite; curtains billowed and flapped like canvasses on a sailing ship.   Crowther stood by the room's door, motioned for Clayton to enter but said nothing.

Clayton took in the scene. 'Bloody hell.' He moved slowly watching his tread careful where his foot came down. The central window in the large bay was broken and protruding through it was a large tree branch; trapped between the dressing table and the branch, the curtain flapped about like an old frustrated woman and resting precariously on the splintered branch of the tree was the corner of a huge mirror frame. Staring up from the bed below the mirror was a blood-soaked corpse, broken glass all around and a shard of mirrored glass embedded in the throat. 'Is that who I think it is?'

WILSON SENSED the search had been called off for the night. Only the wind whistling above the edge of the snow-filled ditch buzzed around his head. He was aware that for the second time that night, his mind was clear. He had to get off the moors, to act fast whilst his tracks stood a chance of being covered by the relentless snow.

Using the collapsed side of the bank, Wilson crawled over the edge and followed the direction of the searcher who, barely an hour earlier had fallen so close beside him. Making slow but steady progress towards the petrol station he bent his head against the wind and headed for the forecourt lights – his only beacon in the howling stormy night.

Several freighters were parked by the main building, their cabs covered in snow, their drivers sleeping off the storm behind misty windscreens. Others stood by the diesel pumps filling their tanks ready to continue their journey. When a police van appeared from behind the petrol station's main building, Wilson crouched by an advertisement board;

his mind lucid, he watched as two officers got out to question drivers filling their tanks. He knew the score – they would search each truck, question every road user in order to track him down. He opted for one vehicle – waited for the driver to be allowed to move on and crept down to the stop sign by the highway. There was little traffic that night but as the police were on alert, he knew the drivers would obey the code. Avoiding the truck's beam, Wilson took position by the junction and waited for the vehicle to stop, penknife open and ready for use.

CLAYTON STUDIED the huge mirror's frame. 'I suppose he saw death coming.'

'Very droll.'

'Are we safe?'

'Been wondering that myself.' Crowther scrutinized the broken chain, which had once held the mirror's corner. 'Without the glass's weight, it should hold.' He pointed to the window, 'As long as the branch doesn't move that is. The pathology van is on its way. As soon as I get him out of here, you can make the area safe.' He checked his watch. 'We'll have to take him to Macclesfield of course. Patterson wants us to use the name he used here.'

'And what was that?' Clayton struggled to stem the tears filling his eyes.

'I knew you'd find this amusing.'

'Sorry Crowther; I really am trying to be professional; and I don't find it amusing: I find it bloody hilarious. You've made my night. Just look at him. And did you know? These frocks – these fancy silky frocks are manufactured by a bloke Hammond tried to drive out of business – poor sod, now he's lost a bloody good customer.'

Clayton wiped away the tears. 'Go on – put me out of my misery, what name does Titzy MacLovely call himself?'

'Maud Sinclair.' Crowther joined in the mirth when Clayton doubled over with laughter, 'I agree Clayton, he looks nothing like a Maud, does he?'

'No – he looks like the tosser he's always been. I've not laughed so much for ages, can't tell you how much this has made my day. I suppose it's got to be kept secret.'

'Afraid so, it appears Superintendent Hammond was involved in fraud.'

'Are there any papers here, is that what Patterson wants me to find?'

Crowther nodded. 'You'll find there's a safe behind the lounge mirror.'

'For such an ugly bugger, he's got a lot of mirrors in this place.'

'*He* didn't think he was ugly. This was his fantasy, not cheap either, like you pointed out, those *frocks*, as you call them, are very costly as is the underwear and the shoes, made to measure, goodness knows who he trusted to make them, probably someone in London. And there are hundreds, probably thousands of pounds worth of jewellery.'

The van arrived taking Hammond's body to the morgue leaving Clayton to arrange for the mirror to be removed from the ceiling, the safe to be opened and the house sealed up.

JOSHUA OPENSHAW topped up Reggie Spencer's glass with cider, took a deep breath and went over the plan again. 'You've done well Reggie, these pics are good, the kids are a perfect likeness, a bloody perfect likeness, I congratulate you, you've done us proud.'

'Thanks Josh, praise indeed from the Professor.'

Josh could never get used to being referred to as the Professor. 'I'm no Professor, but you've really done your research this time - credit where it's due. Now with regards to tomorrow: You'll meet me at the pick-up point then we'll travel together to St. Joseph's; we have to be there before the Christmas party begins. Do you understand?'

'1.30.'

'1.30. Good man Reggie. I'll bring the kittens.'

'But I thought I'd bring puppies.'

'Not this time - the pet shop man knows you - everyone's on edge at the moment. You'll be pulled in and questioned and we can't have that. You are vital to making this work – when Wilson sees you with what he thinks are his kids – he'll lose it big time. Then we'll have him.'

'They're saying he's dead. Killed in a car crash on the Yorkshire Moors.'

'They're lying. Like they refer to him as Detective Inspector when he isn't, another lie made up by the newspapers. Wilson's a survivor – trust me – he'll come to us. Now, I'll go over the plans again. I need to know you won't let me down.'

'I promise Josh, I'll not let you down.'

'And these girls,' Josh pointed to the photos, 'you're sure they're not scared of you? It's important Sergeant Wilson sees you and them together – really close. Do you understand?' Reggie leered showing yellow-brown teeth.

STREET CLEANERS were busy in Market Street. They didn't appear to be hampered by the slushy snow as they gathered cigarette ends, lollypop sticks and other debris from the gutter onto giant-sized shovels. They looked up when Barber drove by with what seemed to be a dignitary sat in the back of the Humber and gave a curious smile when Clayton saluted them. Clayton had had a good night: he patted the boxes of damning evidence tucked safely by his side. These documents, Clayton knew were too dangerous to leave at the station. He would take them home and read them through before handing them into Patterson's care.

There were files with transcripts – both original and falsified. Proof not only of Hammond's guilt but that of his involvement with other, more senior officers serving in the Crown Prosecution Service. A law firm was implicated in cover-ups for gangsters and politicians. Clayton sat back allowing his thoughts to fall systematically into place and for all those revelations that clamoured for his attention, it was Alice's smile that came to the fore.

SUPERINTENDENT PATTERSON was first in the Criminal Investigation Department with Detective Constable Davies arriving five minutes later.

Davies was disturbed to find Clayton not at his desk.

'Morning Davies,' Patterson's voice floated softly from the open door of Hammond's old office. Another thing Davies found unsettling, the Super's door wedged open and a gentle polite voice emitting through it.

'Mornin' Sir,' Davies took off his overcoat, folded it over the back of the spare chair and rubbed his hands together. He headed to the corner sink to fill the kettle. It was hot.

'There's fresh tea in the pot Davies, help yourself.'

The boss making tea – what next?

'Er, thanks Sir. Nippy out there, nowt er nothing like an'ot, er a hot cup of tea to warm you up,' suddenly feeling uncomfortable with chit chat, 'that's wot me mam says, anyway.'

'Always heed the words of wisdom Davies.' Patterson turned the page of the file he was studying. 'Tell me Davies, why are there hand drawn comic books in the file of the missing girls?'

'Mr Dean, the supervisor of the Parcel Depot brought 'em in.'

'I see.' Out of the standard evidence box Patterson pulled a batch of six books held together with an elastic band and laid them on top of his desk. He slid off the band. Davies opened the top drawer of his desk, took out another two. Patterson looked up. 'There's more?'

'D. I. Clayton said to read 'em, find out if there was owt, er anything alarming we should know about. Yer see Sir, David MacLean drew 'em, made up the stories for the kids he babysat.'

'And was there?'

'Was there what?'

'Was there anything alarming?'

'No, well, as long as yer don't mind aliens from outer space, human flesh eating monsters that live in green swamps, and mad emperors ruling the universe, no.'

'Nothing alarming there then,' Patterson flicked through the books, stopped at the centre page, a cartoon of a space ship's cockpit, futuristic instruments being manned by children. 'Why are the characters mostly kids?'

'Mr Dene said it was MacLean's way of communicating with those in his care.' Davies took the books he'd finished reading and showed Patterson the cartoon of a space ship's captain. 'See Sir, this kid is really Mr Dene's oldest, and this,' Davies flicked a few pages, 'is Mr Dene's little girl, she's a princess in this story with powers to read thoughts. She's too big for this kind of thing now, but the kids kept the books, read 'em over again they liked 'em so much.'

'Because MacLean personalised them?'

'Yeh – what kid wouldn't like to be captain of a space ship?'

'Have you given D.I. Clayton your view of the books?'

'Yeh, he demanded I read 'em straight after Mr Dene brought 'em in.'

'So you've read these?' Patterson indicated those on his desk.

'Yes Sir.'

'And the main characters are the children of the Parcel Depot's personnel?'

'Yes Sir, and their dads, and in one story their granny plays the evil sorceress.'

'I don't know whether to be alarmed or not Davies.' Patterson rose from his chair. 'Is it normal for a grown man to play with comics?'

'D.I. Clayton thinks MacLean used his talent to talk and listen to Mr Dene's children in a way he couldn't do normally, they wrote stories too which MacLean added to the books. Mr Dene says all the kids MacLean babysat are doing well at school, really well.'

'Does that make him less alarming?'

'D.I. Clayton ses the little girls, especially the older one, Audrey, are very capable of escaping from MacLean any time they want.'

'And is that what you think?'

'I know what the paper's are sayin' but I agree with D.I. Clayton Sir, David MacLean is clever and deceived us all, but 'e only did it because 'e 'ad to. Acting Detective Inspector Wilson remains a real threat to those kiddies.'

'Yes, well perhaps the solution to that might be found buried on the Pennine Pass some time today.'

'Aye Sir.'

As was arranged the previous night, Barber pulled up outside Clayton's home at precisely 7.30 a.m. The Detective Inspector was ready, waiting at the door whilst the Humber was backing up the driveway. Between them, they loaded the boxes onto the back seat.

'Superintendent Patterson telephoned earlier, he said he doesn't want anyone touching this stuff until they've been vetted by Minshull Street.'

'Hope that doesn't mean we've been vetted behind our backs.'

Barber laughed. 'Makes no odds to me Sir, wife had me vetted three years ago.'

'You've worked for Patterson a long time now, is he as good as they say he is?'

'He's a bloody good copper, if that's what you're asking?'

'I remember him from years back, when I returned from Singapore. Got to work in the same department but unfortunately; not with him.' Clayton stared at the dark streets, wintry and cold, so unlike his memory of the Far East. 'Patterson had a reputation even in those days for good detection work.'

'Still has,' Barber said turning the car onto Deansgate, Christmas lights lifting the morning gloom. 'He drums it into so many recruits, tells them that there's no easy solution to solving a crime.'

Clayton laughed. 'That's what I recall about him. I remember how he stuck up for me once when I was taking flack for keeping every scrap of paper and filing it – even

173

after the case had been closed.' He rubbed his chin, fond memories drifting through his mind. 'Do you think they'll allow him to stay at Lever Street?'

Barber drove into the car park, gliding past the ever-present newspaper reporters camping around the entrances. 'There's a lot of clearing up to do Sir, I think Superintendent Patterson will be with you for quite a while.'

'Good – you'd better let him know we've brought in the goodies.'

THE DESKS of Detectives Parker and O'Brien had been moved into Clayton and Davies's section to accommodate space, which was needed to house the new files brought in from various departments of Lever Street Police Station.

Parker carried his meagre box of belongings across the room, placed them ceremoniously on the newly polished desk and sat down.

'D.I. Clayton won't like *that* Sir,' Davies said pointing to Parker's new pint sized mug.

'Why? Ian's not a man to scoff at a decent pair of tits.'

'Not the tits Sir, the size of the mug.'

'I pay my dues like everyone else – and I don't take milk.'

'No – but ya slurp. We heard ya slurp from yer old desk. Tell yer, he'll not like it – just thought I'd let yer know, that's all.'

'You're wrong Davies, Ian's a man of the world. Anyway, professional tea tasters slurp. It's the proper way to appreciate a good blend. Ian should know that, being as he spent his National Service where they grow it – anyway where is he? Heard he'd trapped off at the dogs last night.'

'Won a few bob – if that's what yer mean.'

'Aye – that an' all, so where is he?'

'Dunno all of it, but summat 'append last night – that's why he didn't collect 'is winnings.'

'The mysterious case - why didn't you go with him?'

Davies lowered his voice, 'Super sent Barber with a car. It brought Clayton back half an hour a go, they're having a meeting up in the conference room.'

'I bet it'll be about Hammond's suspension,' Parker said fondling his giant sized mug. 'Hope it takes a long time. I like the office without that nasty fat git bawling his head off every five minutes.'

'An' I 'ope they find Wilson under twenty feet of snow – dead as the butcher's meat.'

'What's happening with that fella sent down because of Wilson fiddling the evidence? Papers say his mother's going nuts – blames going to prison turned her son's mind, says he knows where MacLean's got Wilson's girls.'

'The Super's looking into it. He's got people finding out what Openshaw did during 'is prison sentence. They say 'e's known as the Professor 'cos of all the writin' an' studying he did.'

'If he's as clever as they say, perhaps he really does know where MacLean is.'

Davies shrugged his shoulders. 'Can't see why the man's bothering, 'e's got a pile of qualifications, why ruin all that over owt that's not his concern?'

'Your not thinking straight – Openshaw's got a criminal record, one that carries a sex offender's tag, even if he were Einstein – he'd never get a job using those certificates.'

'Then 'e knows that?'

'Bloody sure he does, you should be asking what's he really after?'

175

'Revenge? Well 'e's got it: if Wilson's dead. Openshaw's got nowt to grouse about any more.'

TEACHERS AT St Joseph's primary school placed tables end-to-end whilst others unfolded cloths to cover them. The seasonal snow had brought mixed blessings for the Christmas end of term. There were those teachers who took delight in drawing snowflakes and found pleasure in actually showing the children how to compare the artwork with the real thing.

Whilst for others, the cold snap brought the misery of threatened burst water pipes, iced-over bedroom windows and treacherous travelling conditions.

It was for this reason that Miss Atherton, the primary school's head mistress, had allowed those who needed to travel, could, if they wished to, finish a day earlier than scheduled. After all, she reasoned, everything had been done, the Nativity play had been a great success and the carol service got a standing ovation from the invited grandparents: so, after the party, she felt the school could cope with a skeleton staff and of course, she had kind uncle Reggie, as the children called him, who had promised to be on hand to help.

What an absolute blessing that man was. Pity his disturbing little habit was so distasteful, but otherwise, an absolute blessing.

CLAYTON STRETCHED his arms above his head. Sitting for hours was not his scene. Patterson read the body language.

'Go get some lunch Clayton, it's 12 noon.'
'Am I needed here this afternoon?'

'No – you should be grateful you had little to do with any of this. From now on the special investigation lot will be interviewing only those implicated.'

'All this requires a different kind of detecting – not sure I'd want to do it. I don't like enemies from within – those supposedly to be on our side.'

'None of us do – trouble is, this is deep rooted and involves those at a very senior level – not just the ranks like Jenkins. It's been going on a long time, since the war, probably before it.' Patterson stretched his limbs, 'Like you, I'm going to be glad to hand it over to the experts.'

'The barrister, William Gould, will he be given sight of the evidence found in Hammond's dossier?'

'Why do you ask?'

'Wilson was brought in by Hammond to ensure witnesses kept to their false statements. Those stories gave Alfredo Boss fake alibis, or proof his cargo was new machinery instead of worthless scrap metal, crucial stuff when swindling the insurance companies out of thousands of pounds.'

'William Gould doesn't need our help, he's quite capable of fighting for the Insurers. The witnesses should have no fear now that Hammond and Wilson are out of the picture.'

'I don't agree Sir, Alfredo Boss is more than able to lean on witnesses; my concern is the trial itself. It's set for the end of March and some of this,' he gestured towards the stack of files, 'could ensure a conviction. Will any of it be made public before then?'

'I doubt it.'

'Shame.' Clayton straightened his collar and tie, reached for his jacket and began to don it.

'I understand your concern,' Patterson closed the folder. 'But very senior officers are mentioned in these

177

papers. It's obvious to me that Hammond documented everything for his own insurance should he be threatened at any time.' Patterson stacked the folder on top of the pile. 'We can't risk any of this becoming public until it comes to trial – and that will take months, perhaps years.' He held open the palms of his hands. 'It's the law – we police officers merely enforce the law – but those who will sift through this are the law. The very law we're paid to enforce.'

'We have plenty of laws Sir, but what we're lacking at the moment – is justice.'

'Couldn't agree with you more – I know this is sickening,' gesturing towards the files, 'but don't lose faith Ian, justice will prevail.'

'And what of those poor people – those who witnessed a crime being committed only to fall foul of Hammond and his thugs? Where's the justice for them?'

'I don't have an answer Ian. Like you, I'm just a policeman.'

JOSHUA OPENSHAW walked the length of the playing fields, judging the distances between the boating lake and the bushes. His gaze stopped at the upturned rowing boats stacked away for the winter. To one side stood a little hut covered in snow where during the season, you paid the man to hire the boats. Ducks dabbled under the frozen edges of the water.

Josh surveyed the scene, made notes of the position and of the direction of fresh footprints, especially those around the boat-hire hut – dare he allow his heart to flutter? He turned his attention to the school building that bordered the park. From his viewpoint, he could see the windows were lit with yellow light, and decorated with twisted crepe paper. The activity inside was of teachers and ladies in overalls, dinner ladies he thought, carrying plates of sandwiches, jugs of orange juice and bowls of red jelly. After scanning the hut one more time he placed the binoculars into the van's cubbyhole and checked his watch. Not long now he prayed.

'SIR?' DAVIES ran into the conference room. 'Sorry Sir, but we've had a message from Joshua Openshaw – delivered by hand – the desk Sergeant took it minutes ago. It's for D.I. Clayton.' Davies looked around the huge room. 'I thought 'e was 'ere.'

Patterson rubbed weariness from his eyes. 'What does the message say?'

'It says Wilson will show up today at 1.30 by the boating lake in Platt Fields.'

Patterson rose from his chair, grabbed his jacket and thumbed in the direction of the toilet. 'Check in there, D.I. Clayton might've paid a visit, I'll get uniform officers together.'

'No – sorry Sir, forgot to say – Openshaw said no blue uniforms.'

Patterson froze. 'Are you saying Openshaw has actually located Wilson's children?' Clayton had briefed him on the elder girl being terrified of police uniforms. Openshaw would know this; his research notes confirmed he'd studied Wilson's private life including that of his failed marriage and domestic violence. 'Davies?'

'Yes Sir?'

'Is it possible that Openshaw knows Wilson intimately? I mean can he read Wilson's mind?

'Dangerous thing to do if yer askin' me Sir, Wilson's got a mind like a riprap and it don't take much to light the fuse.'

'Quite.'

Down the corridor a door opened, Clayton appeared and stared at Patterson and Davies stood together.

'What's going on?' he asked.

THE NEWSPAPERS had been running the story in the evening editions for two consecutive days. Local papers keen to get onto the subject, printed their version of what they knew about Sergeant Wilson from Filey Road Police Station, so all in all Wilson's name was mentioned everywhere, even B.B.C. radio featured an article with an interview given by Joshua Openshaw's mother.

In it she stated that the crime with which her son was wrongly convicted should not have carried such a long sentence. Not one of the children playing in the park that day said they had been interfered with. Yet Wilson had set up a team to trap a prowler reported days earlier who had exposed himself in front of some children. The trap involved two policemen with cameras.

Mrs Openshaw said her son carried a wounded pigeon in his arms. One that had been found by children playing near the tennis courts and brought to the attention of her son. He told them he would care for it, said he intended to take it home. More children crowded around asking what had happened to the bird, her son was telling them it had a broken wing, he had mended birds' wings' in the past, so reassured the children it was in safe hands.

The police doing the surveillance saw nothing wrong, but photos were taken of her son surrounded by children and stood by the bushes where the flasher had been. Children with horrified expressions were pictured around him. Wilson published the photograph asking for the man in the picture to come forward, to help with enquiries, purely elimination purposes the paper said, so Joshua walked into the police station upon which, he was held and charged with using abusive language and attacking two officers.

Mrs Openshaw said her son had been sent to prison on trumped up charges and this had driven him mad. 'All he keeps saying since he got out is one day he'll find Wilson's girls and take them to Old Ernie's den.'

'What and where is Old Ernie's den?' asked the interviewer for the B.B.C.

'I've no idea – but Sergeant Wilson knows,' she paused for effect, 'and it's not a place to take little girls. Tell Sergeant Wilson his girls will be found in Old Ernie's den and please be quick, if not for my boy's sake for the sake of those little girls.'

'But Mrs Openshaw, Sergeant Wilson is presumed dead.'

'Then God help those little girls.'

CHAPTER FOURTEEN

'BROWN SES the messenger looked nowt like Openshaw – a little fella with 'orrible teeth.'

Davies was briefing Clayton as best as he could. 'That'll be Reggie Spencer,' Clayton said, 'he and Openshaw did time together. Openshaw mentions him a lot in his studies: says he too was wrongly convicted through Wilson's over zealous detecting procedures.'

'Never 'eard it described like that. When he flew at MacLean there were no detecting procedures in evidence.'

'Aye – how did he get away with it? There was no Hammond to help him there, Wilson was on his own.'

'Praps 'e learnt from his old master 'ow to cook the books.'

'Aye perhaps he did.'

Patterson returned: he checked his watch. 'Okay, Brocklehurst has got some of the lads to dress in civvies. I want Parker and O'Brien with you Davies, try to look casual – like you're taking the dog for a walk.'

'We getting a dog?'

'Ignore O'Brien's little jest – this is serious.' Patterson looked it, 'We're going to do something unheard of, but if it comes off we will have averted a major calamity taking place.' He checked his watch again. 'In fifteen minutes two builders' vans will pull up outside the King's Head pub. We pile in and from then on its all ad-lib.'

BY THE gates of St Joseph's primary school Father Christmas handed a balloon on a string to each child arriving to attend the Christmas party. Behind him, a clown with orange hair blew long balloons and made them into poodles, swans and sausage dogs.

Mums, Grannies and Granddads stopped to watch the impromptu performance and when Father Christmas asked for a volunteer to hand out the balloon creations and assist the clown, a little girl ran forward. She bore an uncanny resemblance to Audrey Wilson, though in truth she was only seven years old. Father Christmas gave the little girl a box containing the long balloons and she took her place by the clown. Soon the playground entrance dazzled with balloons bobbing against the grey-white snow. Reggie Spencer came into view. He pushed a painted wooden cart inside of which was a large wicker basket. He stopped by the gate and took a kitten from his inside pocket. He bent down to a little girl who bore a striking resemblance to Linda Wilson and invited her to stroke the tiny creature.

A howl of rage filled the air.

The gathering of Mums, Grannies and Granddads turned their eyes towards the howl and saw a man running from the boat lake. He crossed the football ground and was heading towards them. Instinctively, they gathered their loved ones around them and made for the school building.

The clown lifted the lid of the large basket and more than a dozen pigeons flew from it – they circled above the running man; the flapping of their wings drowning his cries of rage. Again they circled; searching and finding their directional instinct before heading east.

D.C. O'Brien ran from his position by the goal post and caught Wilson side on. But Wilson was travelling like a locomotive, eyes fixed on Reggie and the little girl by his side, he swiped a right arm to O'Brien's stomach winding the lad and causing him to double up. Coming from the left side, Davies caught up with Wilson and dove for his legs, bringing him crashing down. D.I. Parker leapt from the right and held him fast. Others ran from the bushes securing Wilson's capture.

Barry Brocklehurst pushed back the fur-trimmed hood and watched the scene from the school gate. For some unfathomable reason he felt a sense of great pity for the man held handcuffed between Parker and Davies. Patterson caught B.B.'s expression, 'Look at poor O'Brien bent double just from the man's hand. Think what he'd have done to Reggie or what he did do to a five year old child once.'

'Yes Sir, but look at him. Some think he's a hero; others a monster. What's going to 'appen to 'im?'

'I'll do everything I can to have his treatment re-started.'

'E'll not like that Sir.'

'He'll have no choice if he ends up in Broadmoor.'

Inside the school, children were enjoying their Christmas party knowing little of the drama in the park's playing field or why the clown willingly packed up his balloons to accompany the policemen to the station.

THE MOMENT the Land Rover's familiar sound came, Mrs Openshaw looked up from her fireside chair and tried to control the ache burning in her heart. She had to be hopeful for the future but even so, it was hard to set about making tea for her returning son.

Two boys: physically so alike yet mentally poles apart.

She returned Jacob's greeting as it echoed through the huge farmhouse and began to butter bread, warm and fresh from the oven. One son left behind, the other eager to be in the pigeon loft. His thoughts only on making it ready for the return of his beloved birds.

Silently she sent a prayer for Joshua, knowing what he had planned to do and understanding why. Knowing Joshua had given himself up to the police: just as he'd done years ago when no crime had been committed. Knowing Joshua had gone to gaol because Jacob would never survive the sentence; knowing Joshua was loading livestock into a truck sixty miles away when that dreaded photo in the park was taken. Knowing all of this – She had to have faith. Joshua's plea rang in her mind – keep hopeful, Josh had said, we'll get through it – I promise.

The door to the kitchen opened and Jacob filled the hole; Betty wiped her hands on her apron and embraced her soft hearted, soft headed boy.

''Ad a good trip Jake?'

'Yeh mam – Josh said he'd let me pigeons off for me – said yer needed me 'ere so a come 'ome as fast as a could.'

'Good lad.'

'Is ev'rything okay Ma? Josh sed a were to look after ya?'

'Everything's fine – Josh's got studies to do. Y'know, like when he went away from us – well he's got more learnin' to do – that's all.'

185

SUPERINTENDENT PATTERSON sat in on the interview of Joshua Openshaw but as planned, he left Detective Inspector Clayton to conduct the questioning.

Traces of greasepaint lined the furrows of Openshaw's brow making him look more tragic than clownish. He sat back in the chair – his broad shoulders at ease as he waited for the process to begin; confirming to Davies his identity, but refusing the offer of cigarettes.

'Why the charade?' Clayton opened.

'Spur of the moment, there were two things Reggie and I needed to do. One was to clear the way for a retrial and the other was to grab Wilson before someone silenced him forever. It was the events of the last week that brought things to a head.'

Patterson looked up from the page of the document he was reading, made no comment and returned to the papers on his knee.

'I knew Wilson had left Yorkshire,' Openshaw continued, 'but didn't know why.' He looked across to where Patterson sat, his eyes falling on the document. 'I'd been trying to trace Kathleen and the girls,' he continued; distracted by the paper on Patterson's knee, 'but she simply vanished. What's that you're reading? Looks like psychology jargon.'

Patterson looked up. 'It is,' he said before looking down, eyes focused on the page once more.

'The charade,' Clayton prompted, 'you were telling us why it was necessary to perform all that make-believe outside the school.'

'Only way to lure Wilson.' Openshaw explained. 'Inspector, I'm bloody desperate. Wilson falsified evidence against me – made it so watertight that all legal attempts to have it re-examined have been thrown out.'

Clayton inhaled audibly. 'We can see you have a serious problem. We could probably sympathise with your plight but none of us can understand why you went to such lengths to attract attention.'

'Oh come off it Clayton, I hear you're a clever cop. I even betted on you going along with the charade: even to allowing an officer to dress up as Father Christmas.'

Patterson looked up, Clayton flashed him a side-glance.

'Ahh,' Openshaw gleaned. 'My mistake - the Super fixed it.'

Openshaw sat forward, his eyes flicking from Clayton to Patterson. 'One of you had doubts,' he accused, 'thought Wilson wouldn't appear – wondered whether I *did* have the girls hidden in some filthy den after all. You had to go along with my charade to find out.' He sat back. 'The plan was to capture Wilson alive. It worked and now perhaps Wilson will get the treatment he needed years ago.' Openshaw leant forward again. 'Without a retrial, my life is ruined. I need Wilson to put it right but he must be sane to do it. Or,' he said, sitting back in his chair, 'it must be proven he was insane when he had me sent down. Either way, I want that retrial.'

CHAPTER FIFTEEN

WILSON TOOK the offered cigarette and put it to his lips. Johnson flicked open the lighter. Yellow flame lit the hollow cheekbones of his former colleague. He waited while the cigarette was lit pulled the flame back and lit his own.

He inhaled. 'It's for the best Mike.'

'Yeh.'

'You heard about Hammond carking it?'

'Yeh.'

''E was a crafty old sod? Y'know, not one of us knew about his yer know, secret place.'

'Nah.'

'They'll get you right y'know. Won't be like it used to be, honest mate, they'll get yer right properly this time.'

'Yeh.'

'And look,' Johnson pushed an envelope towards Wilson, 'got'cha Ronson back. Forensic found it trapped in Jim Whittaker's Jag an' Superintendent Patterson said I could give it yer – go on, open it, still works.'

Wilson stared at the envelope made no movement other than taking a drag of his cigarette. Johnson did the honours – gently tipping out the Ronson watching it glistened under the ceiling light. 'See,' he said, 'not a scratch. And there's the inscription from yer mates in Leeds; remember?' Johnson pushed the lighter into Wilson's empty hand. 'You've got plenty of good mates Mike. Don't ever forget it.'

Wilson looked up – eyes haunted and hollow, just like his cheekbones.

DAVIES CARRIED two mugs of steaming tea across the room and placed one on the corner of Clayton's desk, the other he carried to his own. He put the rim to his lips, blew cold air across the top and closed his eyes ready to enjoy the sweet brew.

'Don't even think about it.' Clayton cut through the quiet of the room. No need for explanation – he sensed Davies had taken the hint and continued to re-examine items gathered during the investigation of the road traffic accident and abduction of Wilson's children.

Davies took a noiseless, tasteless sip – looked across to Parker's desk and saw the mirth ripple across his lips. Davies opened his mouth to speak thought again and closed it.

Parker filled the silence. 'Who'd've thought,' he said to no one in particular, 'Who'd've thought Hammond was a cross-dresser?'

Clayton looked up. 'Aye? Kept it secret didn't he. Come to think of it, we should've guessed with his smooth skin and close shaves.'

'Had a few of them all right.'

'And 'is nails,' said Davies, 'always summat not right about the Super's nails.'

'How come *you* got the job?' Parker ignoring Davies, addressing Clayton directly, 'You're not Vice, should've been me.'

'You weren't around I suppose.'

'Nor were you.'

'That's true.' Clayton's eyes began to water and his throat dried up; the memory of Dr Crowther's warning about discretion oozing away. 'I suppose there were reasons why Vice didn't handle it,' he croaked, 'anyway you didn't miss much,' he lied, 'and most of the details have leaked out courtesy of the Macclesfield press, so there was no problem?' He turned away trying and failing to hide the tears of pent up hysteria filling his eyes.

Parker's missile hit Clayton on the back of his head. Clayton bent double let out a howl of laughter, picked up the book titled *Safety in the Workplace* and threw it back. Parker caught it, watched Clayton regain his composure and asked, 'Was it *really* that hilarious?'

'Oh man I tell you, it was classic, fucking classic.'

'Bastard.'

Parker threw the book back, Clayton ducked letting out another howl of laughter. The book sailed over Clayton's head and was caught by Davies.

'England's looking for men like you Davies, well caught.' Patterson said upon entering the room. 'Have I missed something here?'

THE TEAROOM was warm and cosy, the air filled with the smell of fresh ham, pastries and cakes. At the table by the window the man held his newspaper in the air, turned the page and re-folded it before placing it onto the linen tablecloth. He read in silence.

The child sat opposite looked a proper picture in her new red coat. She counted pennies, dropping them one by one into a small purse. At the counter, a girl with short-cropped hair ordered the high tea special for three.

Suddenly the little girl at the table shot from her seat, opened the door to the busy main street and ran across the road. Vehicles screeched, the child at the counter ran in pursuit weaving between the slowed down traffic towards her little sister. The cold air alerted the man's attention, he looked up from his newspaper and realised something had happened to the girls. Scant seconds passed by before he took in the street-scene and his eyes fell immediately onto a blonde on the opposite side of the road wearing a tweed coat and a black feather hat. She stopped and turned when a red-coated girl pulled the hem of her coat.

MacLean felt his heart muscles tighten inside his chest. He threaded his way across the street catching up with Audrey and then with Linda who stood looking up at the woman who was not the person she had thought. The woman gave the little girl a strange smile, turned and continued with her errand.

MacLean crouched down, held Linda close; this time, her tears were real, warm against his neck. Clinging to his other side Audrey blinked away her tears to stare after the tweed coated woman wearing a tiny black-feathered hat.

Passers-by side-stepped around the little family huddled together in their deep and secret grief.

CLAYTON FOUND Charlie Faulkner seated by the fire engrossed in the evening newspaper. He slid into a chair next to him. Falkner looked up, his moustache wrinkled into it's customary twisted smile.

'Can't stop,' Clayton said before Charlie could catch the eye of the waiter.

'Too late, he's spotted you. You look like a pint man. Bitter?'

Clayton nodded Charlie placed the order put away his paper and took a sip from his glass of whiskey. 'What can I do for you Inspector?'

'More a case of the other way round.'

'Fire away.'

Clayton wedged a black leather desk diary by the bowl of nuts, picked a handful and popped one into his mouth. Faulkner fingered the leather grain, opened it gingerly and flicked through the pages. 'Where did you get this?'

'Never mind. Is it of use to you?'

'I'll say it is.' Faulkner slid the diary into his brief case. Clayton's pint was put onto the table Charlie watched him take a good swallow. 'Risky business for you.'

Clayton wiped the froth from his upper lip and smiled. 'That depends on how it's handled.'

Charlie's eyes caught the firelight, 'Handling risk is what I do best.'

'So I've heard.' Clayton rose from his seat, drank the remaining ale and placed the froth-coated glass onto the mat. 'Thanks – a good pint.'

'So I've heard.'

Clayton turned to leave – Faulkner coughed, 'Going somewhere special?'

'Taking someone to dinner.'

'Then perhaps you could use these,' Faulkner rummaged in his briefcase, brought out two tickets, handed them to Clayton.

'Thanks Charlie, but I'm not a member.'

'No one is yet. Those are complementary – meant to entice you to join. No harm in giving it a whirl'

'None at all.'

-

DAVIES GAVE O'Brien a nudge and inclined his head towards a crowd of girls filing into the pub. 'What'cha think?'

O'Brien put his pint onto the bar and whistled. 'Bloody hell.'

'Don't stand a chance do we? Lot o'class with those legs, outta our league mate, well out of our league.'

'Don't stand a chance?' O'Brien balked, 'That's defeatist talk.'

'Go on then,' Davies urged, 'invite 'em over.'

O'Brien straightened his tie, adjusted the lapels of his new suit and strolled towards the entrance. Davies watched him from the corner of the bar, studying O'Brien's bird-pulling technique, hoping to learn a few tricks. The women were tall – probably models thought Davies. One stooped to give O'Brien a kiss on the cheek leaving a perfect imprint of lipstick.   The others pointed to the bunch of mistletoe hanging above O'Brien's head, men around the bar were sniggering and when the kisser whispered something in the Detective Constable's ear – he recoiled in horror.

'What 'appened?'

'Drink up.'

Mystified, Davies watched his mate down his pint. Turned to look again at the models but they'd moved into the back room.   Men around the bar settled to telling jokes and drinking. 'Wot went wrong?'

'Not our type – come on, we'll try the Shakespeare.'

'But?'

'But nothing – drink up or leave it.   I'm off.' He looked over his shoulder. 'I don't know what you're finding so bloody funny,' he told the customers around the bar. A woman pushed the men aside and faced O'Brien. She took his handkerchief from his top pocket and wiped away the lipstick.

'Ought to be ashamed of yourselves,' she teased her friends. 'There,' satisfied all the lipstick had been removed she added, 'didn't you read the placard dear, the one by the door?

Davies left most of his beer, gave O'Brien's sleeve a tug and stood by the entrance. He didn't need to read any placard, he was learning fast. Voice was too low, too baritone for his taste. 'Come on,' he called to O'Brien. 'Let's get out of 'ere.'

WILLIAM GOULD flicked through the pages of the pocket diary.

'You can't say where you found it?'

'You know I can't.'

'Yes, yes I understand you have to keep your informers anonymous - but this information isn't any odd snippet. It's got the dates and times Alfredo Boss scuttled his boats and look here,' Charlie had never seen Gould so excited, 'we've even got the fuel delivery note Alfredo used to set fire to his warehouse. These back up the original statements given by Pino's family and those of poor Mr Lloyd.'

'Made more valuable by the name of the diarist.'

'I know – but why? Why risk keeping something this toxic?'

'Insurance. When will you learn the ways of the real world?'

'But a senior partner of Neilson Crane shouldn't need insurance.'

'When you're dabbling your toes in shark-infested waters William, you need all the insurance you can get.'

BRAVING THE chilled air, Mancunians dressed to kill packed the pubs, clubs and theatres. Christmas lights reflected in the pavements left glossy from the melting snow and in Albert Square, the seasonal tree bowed and swayed in the icy breezes.

They'd never had it so good!

Alice's smile warmed Clayton's soul. She placed her arm into his and stepped into the fast pace of his gait. 'What've you got planned?'

He sucked in the cold air. 'Daren't tell you.'

'I mean, where're we going?'

'Your choice, if you fancy, we could go for Italian food?'

'Or?'

'Or.' Clayton pointed to the skyline above Piccadilly Gardens, 'We could go there.'

Alice looked across to where new offices were under construction. Nestled between these edifices was a tower building with a gigantic oyster glowing from its roof.

'Pearls?'

'If you fancy – its new but very smart they say.'

'Oh I fancy.' Eyes dancing: falling easily into his speedy pace, 'I fancy alright.'

23167108R00117

Printed in Poland
by Amazon Fulfillment
Poland Sp. z o.o., Wrocław